HIS GRUMPY CHILDHOOD FRIEND

CIDER BAR SISTERS, BOOK 2

JACKIE LAU

First edition: October 2020
ISBN: 978-1-989610-18-3

Editor: Latoya C. Smith, LCS Literary Services

Cover Design: Flirtation Designs

Cover photograph: Depositphotos

CHARLOTTE, WILL YOU MARRY ME?

Charlotte Tam stared at the words on the scoreboard and felt a prickle of anxiety.

But there were thousands of people in the Rogers Centre, and that message was likely for another Charlotte.

Yes, Brad Tomson talked loudly, stole the blankets, and told her to smile more, but she loved him. Her boyfriend would never do anything as stupid as a scoreboard proposal at a baseball game.

Right?

Such a proposal was, quite literally, the stuff of her nightmares.

She'd first seen a scoreboard proposal on TV when she was six. She'd been a Toronto Blue Jays fan for as long as she could remember, thanks to her father, and she'd been watching the game with him, her little sister, and her friend Mike. Her father had explained what was happening, and she'd been horrified. To have so many people watching while you kissed someone? She didn't even like when people sang "Happy Birthday" to her. More than anything, though, that proposal had made her think of show-and-tell, which she hated doing at school.

Charlotte might have forgotten about the proposal, but that night, for some reason, she'd had a nightmare about it, and she'd had many similar nightmares since then. Other people might dream of showing up at school in their underwear, but Charlotte's subconscious came up with variations on a public proposal at a ballgame. In one version of this dream, a cartoon prince rode up on a white horse, in front of tens of thousands of people, and she was clad in only a seashell bra, and everyone was laughing at her when her name flashed on the screen. In another version, the proposal was followed by a vicious monster attack.

Why did she keep dreaming about this? She had no idea—her brain worked in strange ways at times—but it meant she'd thought quite a bit about these types of proposals. They were the last thing she wanted.

Hopefully this mysterious person named Charlotte felt differently—

Oh, God.

Brad was getting down on one knee. He'd spilled beer on the floor in the third inning, so it must be sticky.

And, yep, he was holding a ring box in her direction.

She went hot and cold at the same time, and her heart started beating far too fast. She wiped a hand over her sweaty brow, feeling more horrified than she'd ever been in her life. Seriously, this was the worst.

She was the Charlotte on the scoreboard after all.

It wasn't as weird as any of her dreams, but it was equally bad, despite the lack of seashell bra and scary monsters. In fact, being eaten by a monster might be a blessing right now. It would put an end to this humiliation.

"Say yes!" someone shouted from behind her.

"He hasn't even popped the question yet, you idiot," someone else said.

"But it's already on the screen."

Brad looked up at her with a stupid cocky smile.

"Will you marry me?" he asked.

Time seemed to slow, which was awful, since everyone was staring at her and awaiting her response. They wanted Charlotte to say yes and throw her arms around Brad and kiss him—a kiss that would be shown on the large screen in the stadium and probably on TV.

Charlotte and Brad had never talked about marriage, but they'd been together for three years, and she'd thought he was the guy she'd marry. It seemed sensible, even if he had lots of habits that got on her nerves.

But now, she didn't want to say yes.

Because she realized Brad didn't know her, not even a little.

God, how could she have dated him for three years and missed something so obvious?

There had been signs. She could see them now. He'd tried to take her dancing at a club more than once, but she hated the press of bodies, the loud music, and—worst of all—the actual dancing. He'd also planned a cottage getaway with not one, not two, but *three* other couples she didn't know. Not her idea of a good time. Despite her irritation, she'd brushed those things off, told herself they were no big deal.

She'd been pleased when he'd mentioned he had tickets to this game. She liked the Jays. Wasn't it thoughtful of him?

Ha. She didn't think that anymore.

This took the cake. Because anyone who knew Charlotte Tam would realize that she would not want a public proposal at a ballgame, even if they didn't know about her ridiculous dreams.

And Brad did know. One time when they were tipsy, she'd told him about her recurring nightmares and said she hated the idea of such proposals. Apparently, he hadn't thought she was serious. He must have assumed that since she liked baseball, this was the perfect place to propose.

In an instant, all the affection she'd ever had for him evaporated.

"Charlotte," Brad hissed. "Say yes."

She hated him for putting her in this position. If you were going to do a spectacle like proposing at a ballgame, wouldn't it make sense to talk about it with your partner first?

Brad would claim that would have ruined the surprise.

Well, some surprises were fucking terrible.

Everyone was looking at her, either in person or on the screen. Expecting her to say something she'd just realized she could not do.

Charlotte wasn't the sort of person who'd say yes because it was easier.

"Don't break his heart!" someone shouted.

She felt a stab of guilt, but she quickly pushed that aside.

Brad had done something idiotic, and she refused to feel guilty.

She tried to speak, but no words came out. Instead, she just shook her head.

And then she bolted.

She stepped on two people's feet—she would have said sorry, but her voice still wasn't working—then hurried up the stairs and out the nearest exit.

People were shouting at her, but she didn't care.

Brad was probably mortified. Not her problem. She'd thought she loved him, and now all she felt was anger.

How dare he make her nightmare come true.

Charlotte exited the stadium. She kept running, not paying attention to where she was going, just needing to escape, to put as much distance between her and Brad as possible.

There'd been two innings left, and she'd miss them. Goddamn him for ruining the game. The Jays had been losing, but still.

She found herself running west on Queen Street. Why? Where was she going?

Then she remembered. Her friends from university had decided to try a new cider bar on Ossington tonight.

By the time she got to Ossington Cider Bar, which had to be at least three kilometers from the stadium, she was out of breath. She stepped inside and bent over. She must look like a mess in her John Olerud jersey and Blue Jays cap, her hair slicked with sweat.

"Charlotte?" Nicole crouched in front of her, concern on her face. "What happened?"

"Brad proposed."

"I thought you were at a Jays game?"

"He proposed at the Jays game. It was on the big screen and everything."

"Oh, no," Nicole whispered.

Sierra and Rose joined them.

"That asshole," Sierra said when she heard the story.

"Come on," Nicole said, taking one of Charlotte's arms. Rose took the other. "We're going to get you some booze and maybe some dessert. I bet they have something with coffee."

Her friends understood her a million times better than Brad did, that was clear. And he'd been an improvement over her first two boyfriends, who hadn't lasted long.

What was the point of dating when it was just going to end in a nightmare?

As the first sip of cider crossed her lips, Charlotte Tam, who'd secretly dreamed of a small, romantic wedding ever since she was a little girl, swore off dating.

$$[\ 1\ ]$$

Five years later...

CHARLOTTE HATED WEARING PANTS.

Okay, she didn't hate all pants. She liked her comfy pajama pants—she had seven pairs—which she wore to work every day.

She worked from home, in the corner of her living room. It suited her perfectly. Better than when she'd worked in an office and needed to put on proper clothes every day. And have inane small talk around the coffeemaker.

She yanked on her only pair of jeans. Some people thought jeans were comfortable, but Charlotte disagreed. Jeans had a fucking button and a zipper. So restricting.

Next, she put on a bra—yes, an actual bra—and a short-sleeve white blouse, followed by some necklaces that Nicole had picked out for her on a truly painful shopping trip. Finally, a headband.

As a reward for getting dressed, she tossed back another cup of coffee, then put on her Converse shoes, grabbed her purse, and left her apartment for the first time in three days.

Her friends better appreciate the sacrifices she made for them.

She decided to check the mail on the way out. Unfortunately, her neighbor was doing the same thing, and she tried to—horror of horrors—engage Charlotte in a conversation about the weather.

Charlotte didn't know anything about the weather. She hadn't left her apartment in three days, after all.

At last, she made her escape and headed outside. It was, as her neighbor had assured her, a nice day for mid-July. Warm but not as oppressively humid as it sometimes got in Toronto.

Ossington Cider Bar was a short transit ride away. She found her friends on the back patio. They'd all arrived before her today, which was unusual.

"You look great!" Nicole said. "Are those the necklaces I insisted you buy?"

Charlotte had met these women when she was a first-year engineering student at Queen's University in Kingston. Charlotte Tam, Nicole Louie-Edwards, Sierra Wu, and Rose Pang were more than half of the Asian women in their year in engineering, which was about six hundred people. Charlotte, having grown up in the small town of Ashton Corners, was used to being surrounded by white people, but Nicole and Sierra, who'd grown up in Toronto? Not so much.

Charlotte had few friends. Friends involved socializing, and she needed only a limited amount of socializing in her life. A couple of Saturdays a month with these women, who'd known her for over a decade, was the perfect amount.

She studied the cider list. The strawberry Earl Grey, blackberry nectarine, and passionfruit peach ciders were all on tap. Bleh. They were far too sweet. Fortunately, there was a new cider, which was supposed to be crisp and bone dry. Excellent. "Bone dry" was her favorite type of cider, much to Nicole's distress.

When their server came around to give Sierra her beloved Brussels sprouts, Charlotte ordered her cider as well as a burger.

Ossington Cider Bar made delicious juicy burgers, and the fries were excellent, too. She and her friends had been hanging out here regularly since the day of Brad's infamous proposal.

"Amy's not coming today?" Charlotte asked Sierra.

Sierra shook her head. "She's got a date with Victor."

Amy Sharpe—Sierra's housemate—was a recent addition to the group. Charlotte didn't like change, but she did like Amy, even if they were opposites; Amy was perky and cheerful and wore clothes with polka dots and ladybugs.

"It doesn't seem fair," Sierra said. "Amy joined our group and immediately got a boyfriend, and now they're engaged. She's two years younger than us. We're all single at thirty-three."

"I'm still thirty-two," Charlotte pointed out.

"Well, I'm not complaining." Nicole sipped her sickeningly-sweet cider. "I don't want a boyfriend."

"I trust it will happen to me eventually," Rose said.

"You have to get out there," Sierra said. "Make an effort. Last night, I went on my first date in months."

"How'd that go?" Nicole asked.

"Horrible. He wouldn't shut up about how much money he made, but he was a complete cheapskate."

Charlotte agreed with Sierra. If you wanted a relationship, you had to put yourself out there. You couldn't just hope that one day, the right guy would come along.

Case in point: Charlotte had been single for five years and not once had a guy so much as asked to buy her a drink.

Okay, it probably didn't help that she rarely left her apartment, but still.

She knew she had to *try*.

"I think I'd like to date again," Charlotte said.

Three heads snapped toward her.

"But *why*?" Nicole asked.

Because Charlotte, to her secret shame, was a bit of a romantic. Had been ever since her aunt's wedding when she was a little girl. Her mom had given her a wedding coloring book before the special day, and she'd loved it. Back then, she'd wanted to marry a baseball player.

Except her experiences with dating as an adult were, well, not promising.

Charlotte wanted a relationship with someone who understood that she didn't like leaving her apartment on a regular basis. Who understood that getting engaged at a baseball game was the last fucking thing she'd ever desire.

She wanted someone who *got* her and accepted her caffeine addiction, hatred of humanity, and lack of general good nature. A man who didn't tell her to smile more, like Brad had. She wouldn't put up with that shit again.

Unfortunately, in her experience, men didn't like her as she was. Or they thought she was someone she wasn't. Plus, the last time she'd been on a first date was eight years ago.

Eight goddamn years.

The idea of going on another first date made her shudder. A first kiss? Dear God. She was already hyperventilating.

Rose placed a hand on her back. "What's wrong?"

"I want a boyfriend in theory," Charlotte said, "but in practice… Well, dating is painful. How many terrible dates will I have to sit through to find a half-decent guy? And I have no idea how to act on a date. It's been so long since I've been on one." She didn't admit her fear that she would never find a guy who truly liked her.

Charlotte's cider arrived, and she eagerly took a sip. Yes, nice and dry.

"I know what you need," Rose said. "Love lessons."

"Excuse me?" Nicole said. "You think Charlotte should hire someone to teach her how to date?"

"No, she should find a kind male friend to give her some guidance. Go on fake dates with her. Get her used to the idea."

Nicole and Sierra looked skeptical.

"What?" Rose said. "I read it in a book once."

Charlotte sighed. "There's one serious problem. It requires me to have male friends."

She had two men who could possibly be considered friends. One was a colleague from when she'd worked in an office. He was married. The other guy played videogames with her online sometimes. He lived in California and she'd never met him in person.

Neither of those would work.

"Surely we can think of someone," Rose said.

Sierra shook her head. "Sorry, Rose, but this plan is ridiculous. Dating is something you just do, not something you deliberately practice. And practice kissing? That's weird."

Charlotte admitted that it did sound a bit weird, but it appealed to the side of her that was uncomfortable with unfamiliar social situations. She'd been a little shy as a kid, but she wouldn't consider herself shy, precisely, now; she just didn't have a lot of experience with certain things, and she wanted to feel confident on her dates.

But her lack of friends was a bit of an issue. She didn't have anyone she could ask.

Oh, well.

Her food arrived, and she busied herself with pouring vinegar on her fries and putting relish on her burger.

She'd just taken a big bite of her burger when Nicole whispered, "Look at the Asian man sitting by the door. At the table with two white guys. He's hot, isn't he?"

Charlotte chewed slowly as she glanced at the man in question.

And then she dropped her burger.

OMG. It couldn't be.

But she'd know that smile anywhere, even if she hadn't seen it in twenty years.

Once upon a time, Charlotte did have a close guy friend. His family had moved in next door when she was six. Another Chinese family in their mostly-white town. They were the same age, and he'd let her boss him around. They'd both enjoyed drawing, and when she told him she wanted to draw quietly, he'd stay quiet…for the most part. Occasionally, he'd speak, but she hadn't minded because he usually made her laugh.

She didn't reminisce for long, though, because she was distracted by the fact that he looked really fucking good.

He was wearing a polo shirt, holding a pint of cider, and laughing at something his friend said. His features were sharp and grown-up and unbelievably handsome.

Mike Guo. Who would have thought?

And then she remembered she was pissed at him.

His family had moved away when they were thirteen. One day, she'd woken up to see the moving truck pulling away.

He hadn't told her they were leaving. Hadn't attempted to say good-bye. He could have at least written her a letter, right? He would have known her address.

But she'd never heard from him.

Until last December.

Charlotte rarely logged into her Facebook account. She'd had it since university, back when it wasn't yet available to the general public, only college and university students. But she didn't check it often. And so, when she logged in the day before Christmas, she found that Mike Guo had messaged her two weeks earlier.

She'd considered replying, but in the end, she hadn't.

Yeah, she knew it was stupid to be bitter about something that had happened twenty years ago. She really wasn't *that* bitter—it wasn't like she thought of Mike very often—but when she'd seen that message, it had all come rushing back. Her devastation that her only close friend was simply…gone.

So, no, she hadn't replied, though she'd checked his profile and discovered that he, too, lived in Toronto. But the city itself had over two million people, and the GTA was much bigger. What were the odds he'd show up at the cider bar?

"Charlotte?" Sierra said. "You okay?"

"I think it's love at first sight," Rose whispered.

Charlotte jerked her gaze away from Mike. "Love at first sight doesn't exist. No, I know that guy. From Ashton Corners. We went to elementary school together."

"Wait a second," Nicole said. "Is that Mike? *The* Mike?"

Charlotte rolled her eyes. "Yes, it's him."

But, whatever. He was in the past. She didn't need to talk to him.

And then he looked up from his pint, his gaze colliding with hers across the small patio. He immediately said something to his friends and walked over to her.

Of course he did. Because this was Mike. He always wanted to be social, and he had no idea how pissed she'd been at him.

She wiped her mouth and stood up.

"Hey," she said, trying to act all casual.

"Charlotte Tam!" He grinned. "It really is you."

"Yep, it's me. Hi, Mike."

She discreetly checked him out. Like her, he was wearing jeans; unlike her, he probably hadn't complained about having to put on proper pants. He'd been a lanky boy, but he'd filled out since, and he'd been shorter than her at thirteen, but now, he had a good six inches on her. He had laugh lines around his mouth, and the faintest wrinkles at the corners of his eyes.

Her skin felt strangely hot and tingly, but surely that was just because he was her old friend and she hadn't seen him in ages.

And because Charlotte didn't have tons of experience with situations like these, and she couldn't help thinking about the day she'd discovered he was gone, she blurted out, "Why did you leave without telling me?"

She prided herself on telling the truth, on not mincing words, but she hadn't meant to ask that question quite so soon.

Mike wrapped his hand around her upper arm and steered her to the corner of the patio where there were no tables.

It was kind of nice to be touched by him.

"You haven't seen me in twenty years," he said, the corner of his mouth tipping up, "and that's the first question you ask me? Not, 'how have you been, Mike?'"

"Yes." She'd asked the question, so she'd commit to it.

Mike threw his head back and laughed. "Glad you haven't changed." Then he sobered. "I didn't tell you we were moving because I didn't know."

"How could you not know?"

"My parents didn't tell us. They woke us up at five in the morning and said we had an hour to pack up everything important. That was it." He dropped his hand from her arm and clenched it at his side.

"You didn't call me or write to me. Nothing." God, she sounded whiny.

"My parents tore up my letter and forbid me from contacting anyone in Ashton Corners. If I'd tried to call, they would have seen the long-distance charges."

Oh. She blew out a breath.

She should have figured something like this was a possibility. Mike had always hung out at her house; she'd never gone to his. His relationship with his parents hadn't been good, but he'd rarely talked about it. He'd gotten along with everyone, so it had been puzzling that his family seemed to be the exception. And though she didn't know much, she'd known his parents sometimes did things that made no sense whatsoever.

"Look," he said, shoving his hands in his pockets. "I'm sorry about all that. Really, I am. Is that why you didn't reply to my message on Facebook?"

"Yeah. Plus, Facebook sucks, and I'm rarely on there."

"Okay, now that we've gotten that out of the way, can we catch up? What are you up to these days?" He smiled at her.

He was so familiar and different at the same time.

"I studied geological engineering at Queen's. Those are my friends from university." She gestured to her table.

Nicole, Sierra, and Rose were avidly watching her conversation. She gave them the middle finger—they wouldn't be insulted; she did this often—then returned her attention to Mike.

"Now I'm a geophysicist," she said.

"Sounds fancy."

She shrugged. "What about you?"

"I'm a financial planner."

"That must involve putting on nice clothes every day and meeting with lots of clients."

"It does."

She cringed at the thought. "I work from home now, so I can wear pajamas. I'm trying to wrap my head around the idea of you having such a grown-up job like a financial planner."

"What did you imagine me doing?"

"Not sure. Maybe an artist?"

A shadow briefly passed over his face.

"But we were kids," she said. "There were many jobs we'd never considered."

"So true. I wanted to be a baseball player for most of my childhood, but there aren't many people who actually make a living playing baseball."

She couldn't help wondering how Mike's ass would look in a Blue Jays uniform.

Cut it out, Charlotte!

But she did want to start dating again soon, didn't she?

Not that she could imagine dating Mike. He was her childhood friend. They'd drawn side by side and played boardgames together.

However…

She could use a male friend right now. To practice, as Rose had suggested.

Mike Guo would be the perfect person to give her dating lessons. They'd only just spoken for the first time in twenty years, so he didn't know much about her life, just like a potential boyfriend. And she felt comfortable with him. After learning why he'd never told her about his family's move, her anger had dissipated, and it had only taken her a few minutes to feel the ease that she used to have with him. Which she didn't feel around most people.

Although Charlotte didn't know what Mike had been up to for the past two decades, he must have lots of dating experience. He was a sociable, good-looking guy who probably went out a lot.

"Mike, can I ask you a favor?"

"Sure." He leaned in closer. "Go ahead."

"This might sound kind of weird…"

"Anything for you."

She was rather distracted by his words—and his clean, soapy smell—but she kept going. "Can you teach me how to date?"

[2]

"You want me to teach you how to date?" Mike Guo asked his former best friend, trying not to let on how ridiculous and surprising he found this. Trying to act cool, like nothing fazed him.

It was the act he'd perfected as a child. In fact, it was rarely an act anymore; it was natural. But right now, he was definitely faking it.

"Sorry," Charlotte said. "I shouldn't have assumed you were single." She smacked her forehead then grabbed his hand, presumably to look for a ring.

There was no ring.

"I'm not seeing anyone," he said.

"Phew. Because you're my only hope."

He'd just seen her for the first time in years, and now he was her only hope?

He'd always had a little trouble keeping up with Charlotte's mind.

"Right, I'm probably not making any sense," she said. "It's just that I haven't been on a first date in eight years, but I'm hoping to start dating again soon. I could use a friend to take me on some practice dates. Just, you know, so I don't make a fool of myself."

"Eight years?"

There was a story there, but he wouldn't press any further. He didn't like to push people to reveal things they weren't ready to reveal, because he knew what it was like to be on the other end of that.

"I had a bad experience," she said. "I swore off dating five years ago. And now, I could use some help."

The weird thing was, he used to hope that one day, he'd be able to do something gallant for Charlotte. When they were kids, it had felt like she was always the one saving him.

It probably hadn't felt like that to her.

But she'd helped him with his French homework. Shared all her toys with him. Best of all, she'd let him use her box of sixty Laurentien pencil crayons and her watercolors. When they were older, she'd snuck him into her room for late-night boardgames and cookies she'd pilfered from the pantry.

He had lots of friends at school, but he rarely got a chance to see them outside of school. Charlotte was his best friend partly due to geography.

Next door. Very convenient.

Plus, his parents hadn't disapproved of her family to the degree that they disapproved of most people, probably because they were also Chinese, though her family was very, very different from his own.

But the main reason she'd been his best friend was simply that she was Charlotte.

The facial expressions she made now were achingly familiar, though she'd changed, too. She was cute...in a totally grown-up manner. She was wearing a headband, which had been her trademark when she was little, although she'd stopped wearing them by grade seven. But this headband was different from the ones she'd worn back then. Her white shirt was unbuttoned to the tops of her breasts, and he tried not to stare.

And she had a job he didn't understand. Not surprising. She'd always been smart.

When he'd turned twelve, his feelings for her had changed. Sure, she was his friend, but there was also, well, whatever his brain had considered love back then. He shuddered to think of it. He'd known she was too good for him, of course, and he'd never said a word about his feelings.

Now, the first girl he'd ever loved was standing in front of him, looking very pretty and asking him to go on a date with her.

No, a *practice* date.

"You think I'm an expert at dating?" he asked.

"Yes."

"Oh?" He couldn't help smiling. "Why is that?"

"Because…" She gestured at him and her cheeks turned pink.

He leaned forward, just a little. Okay, maybe more than a little, because he could feel her breath, faintly, on his neck, which gave him all sorts of interesting ideas. "Because why?"

"Because!"

"I don't know, Charlotte. I think I'll have to give you zero out of two on your answer. It wasn't satisfactory."

Her eyes flashed. She'd always hated getting bad marks.

"Because you're really hot!"

He let out a bark of laughter and steadied himself on the fence enclosing the patio.

"And when you said 'because why,' you sounded all seductive and shit," she continued. "You clearly know what you're doing. And you're…you." She gestured to him again.

"What do you mean?"

"You were always good with people. I bet you enjoy hanging out with your friends every weekend. Talking to women you find attractive. Unlike me. Until an hour ago, I literally hadn't left my apartment in three days."

Some of what she'd said was true. He looked over his shoulder and waved at Mason and Cody.

But he was very, very inexperienced when it came to relationships. In fact, he had some anxiety when it came to the whole idea of love.

Sure, he'd dated a few women. Briefly. He'd never had anyone he'd call a girlfriend, and it wasn't like he got lots of women into bed without going on dates, either.

You're a loser. You'll never get anywhere in life.

Those unwanted thoughts popped into his head much less often than they used to, but it still happened on occasion, and he'd never been able to entirely shake his amazement that he was a semi-functional, independent adult.

Yet, he was standing beside the girl—the woman—who'd always made him feel like he was okay as he was.

He didn't want to tell her that he actually knew very little about dating, but he was warming to her idea. It would be good to spend more time with Charlotte, and he could certainly use some practice at dating, too.

"Two out of two for your answer," he said. "And yes, we can go on some practice dates."

"You're agreeing to my crazy idea?" Her face lit up.

God. Back in the day, he'd done everything he could to see her light up like that.

"Sure, sounds like fun. How about you give me your number?"

Practice dating, he reminded himself. *Practice.*

Her burger was no longer warm, and her fries were a bit limp, but Charlotte didn't care. She stuffed her face as soon as she sat back down and tried to avoid her friends' curious looks.

Of course, she couldn't do it for long.

"So, what happened there?" Sierra asked. "It sure looked interesting."

"What I want to know," Rose said, "is what he was saying when he leaned in close and you turned pink."

"I did not turn pink," Charlotte protested.

"You totally did," Nicole said, "and you were looking at him like he was an ice cream cone you wanted to lick."

Now *this* was going too far.

Charlotte crossed her arms over her chest. "Was not."

"It was very interesting," Nicole said. "Can't remember you ever looking at a guy that way before, and he sure is cute."

Charlotte glared at her friend.

"Looked like you exchanged numbers," Sierra said. "You have a date next weekend?"

Charlotte would tell her friends the truth, even if she dreaded their reaction. "Remember Rose's idea about love lessons? I asked him to help me."

"You asked him to teach you about love?" Nicole asked, a little too loudly.

"Yeah, why not?"

Her friends all looked at each other.

"Well, you know I thought it was a silly idea," Nicole said. "No offense, Rose."

"None taken," Rose said.

"Me, too," Sierra jumped in. "I can't believe you're actually doing this. And I thought you were mad at him for not telling you his family was leaving town?"

"I was, but he explained it. His parents didn't tell him they were leaving. From the little I know of his parents, it's entirely plausible."

"I think you want to bang him," Nicole said. "Do these lessons involve sex?"

"That's not the plan."

"I know the love lessons were my suggestion," Rose said, "but I don't think love lessons with Mike are a good idea."

"Why not?" Charlotte stuffed a limp fry in her mouth.

"You clearly like him. You should date him for real, rather than going on practice dates."

"Uh-uh. Mike is good-looking, but there was never anything like *that* between us."

"You were only thirteen."

"Date him for real," Sierra said. "I agree. You looked so enamored with him."

"I did not." Charlotte hadn't, had she? It had just been nice to see him again, and conveniently, he was the solution to her problem. Going on practice dates with Mike would ease her back into the idea of dating, and he could give her some tips.

And then, hopefully, she could meet a nice guy. A guy who actually understood her.

Hopefully she wasn't wishing for a llamacorn.

Yes, what she needed was a guy who was more similar to her than Brad. A guy who was also a homebody and also drank six to eight cups of black coffee a day, for example. Brad had been her opposite; that had been her mistake.

She would not make that mistake again.

She'd get extroverted Mike to teach her about dating, but he was all wrong for her. Besides, they used to play with Lego together. She used to sneak Oreos for him. She couldn't imagine dating him for real, though she had, for a split second, thought about kissing him…

"You're thinking about it, aren't you?" Nicole said. "Licking him like an ice cream cone."

"Shut up," Charlotte growled. She'd only been thinking about kissing for research purposes. For practice.

"Ooh," Rose said. "I could use some ice cream."

"Okay, we'll find a guy for you, too." Nicole had a sip of cider.

"No, I mean real ice cream. We'll have one more cider and then head to Treatzz?"

Charlotte thought the spelling of "Treatzz" was an abomination, but they made good ice cream, which you could get sandwiched between cookies or in a bubble waffle. She started salivating at the thought of a bubble waffle stuffed with tiramisu and fig goat cheese ice cream.

"Yep," she said. "That's just what I need." If she was going to bother putting on pants, she might as well have ice cream.

As she finished her cider, her thoughts drifted back to Mike Guo.

What would their first practice date be like?

[3]

"WHO WAS THAT?"

Mike had a sip of his strawberry Earl Grey cider—that really was good shit—before answering Mason's question. "A childhood friend. From when I lived in Ashton Corners."

Mason frowned. "Ashton Corners?"

"A small town on Lake Huron. That's where I spent much of my childhood."

"I thought you grew up in Toronto?" Cody said.

"I went to high school here, but before that, we lived in a small town."

"She was the other Asian kid in your grade?"

"Yup. She also lived next door."

Mike had heard the other neighbors complaining about how Chinese people were taking over the street, just because there were two families next door to each other. Well, the man had used a word other than "Chinese," which Mike had later looked up in the dictionary.

"Anyway, it was good to see Charlotte," Mike said, all casual, as though it had simply been "good" and not the highlight of his week. "Got her number so we can catch up."

He didn't tell his friends about their plans for dating lessons. Nah, he'd keep that between him and Charlotte.

He glanced over at her table. She really did look lovely. She put a fry in her mouth—did she still douse her fries in vinegar? He used to tease her about how she loved vinegar on fries, and salt and vinegar chips.

Mike, on the other hand, was a ketchup guy. Lots of ketchup on his fries. Ketchup chips. That was the way it should be.

"So, Mason," he said. "Where are we off to next?"

Mason always had lots of interesting bars and restaurants he wanted to try, and Mike was happy to go along for the ride.

"Little craft beer bar around the corner." Mason jerked his thumb over his shoulder. "They've got some old pinball machines. It's supposed to have a good atmosphere."

Mike laughed. Dude was always talking about atmosphere and shit like that.

After a couple drinks at the craft beer bar, Mason wanted ice cream. Apparently, there was an amazing ice cream place nearby. Mike doubted it would be open at eleven thirty at night, but when they got there, sure enough, it was open, and there were about a dozen people in line. Mason was going on about their fig goat cheese ice cream when something caught Mike's eye.

Charlotte and her friends were walking out of the ice cream shop. Charlotte had a bubble waffle, curled in the shape of a cone. She stuck her little spoon into her ice cream and slid it into her mouth, and he was mesmerized.

He wondered what else she liked to do in Toronto. How did she spend her time?

"Yo, Mike," Mason said.

Mike turned to his friend, who was now two meters in front of him. Right. He should keep the line moving.

"You also gotta try the olive oil ice cream," Mason said.

Cody made a face. "I don't think so. And please, take off that toque."

Mason touched the gray knit hat on his head. "What's wrong with my hat?"

"It's fucking July. Women are walking around in tank tops and short shorts, and you're wearing a toque like it's January. Plus, you got the plaid shirt, the glasses, the beard, and you're talking about olive oil ice cream. You've turned into such a hipster."

Mike laughed as he watched Charlotte head up the street with her friends. Her ass looked nice in those jeans. What kind of ice cream had she gotten? Did she think olive oil belonged in ice cream?

Would she like it if Mike grew a bushy beard, started wearing toques in the heat of July, and got himself a pair of glasses he didn't need?

Not that he was capable of growing a beard. He'd once tried to do Movember, and two weeks in, people still couldn't tell he was participating.

He hoped Charlotte didn't have a thing for beards, then reminded himself, once again, that they were practice dating, not real dating.

Ten minutes later, Mike made it to the front of the line, and he got a bubble waffle with lemon meringue plus chocolate ginger—no goat cheese or olive oil ice cream for him. The lemon meringue was particularly tangy and delicious. If he hadn't run into Charlotte, it would have been the highlight of his evening.

Mason ordered some kind of smoked bourbon ice cream in addition to olive oil, and Cody disappointed Mason by going to a fancy ice cream place only to order chocolate and strawberry.

They ambled down the street. The air was warm, and the chatter from various conversations drifted toward them on the breeze.

Yeah, Mike was pretty happy with his life, a far cry from how he'd felt a decade ago when—

Oh, shit.

His sister was coming tomorrow.

~

"Your new place isn't very big," Angela said. "I thought you said you were moving to a bigger apartment."

"It *is* bigger," Mike said defensively. "Six hundred square feet. The last place was five-fifty. And I have a den." He gestured to said den.

Angela frowned. "That's not a den. That's a little nook in which you've shoved a desk."

"Whatever. I like it."

"I wouldn't have agreed to stay here for a few nights if I'd known it was so small."

"You and Bailey will have plenty of room in the bedroom. It's a queen bed. I'll sleep on the couch. And Angela," he said. *"Don't."*

One word, but his sister would know what it meant.

Mike had gone no contact with his parents eight years ago, but he hadn't gone no contact with his sister.

He and Angela, who was only a year younger than him, had been forced to compete for scraps of praise throughout their childhood. But he'd felt like there were higher expectations on him, as the oldest child, and she had it easier in comparison. Plus, he'd been considered responsible for some of her fuck-ups. Angela, however, had thought he'd had it easier because he was the son.

In truth, their parents had been emotionally abusive to both of them, but he and his sister still sometimes brought out the worst in each other and resorted to childish conversation. Mike had never quite figured out how to hang out with Angela as an adult, even if she and Bailey were all the family he had now.

Well, there were his aunt and uncle and cousins out in Vancouver, whom he occasionally visited, but they weren't super close.

Bailey was a bit of a mystery to him. His niece was ten, and over the years, he'd tried to do various things with her. Lego.

Boardgames. Catch. The museum, the art gallery. He'd even tried to talk with her about music that was supposed to be all the rage with kids her age. None of those had gone well.

A couple years ago, he'd taken her out for sundaes, but it turned out that Bailey was the only kid in the world who didn't love sweets. Perhaps she'd like olive oil or goat cheese ice cream, though. Hmm.

"Hey, Bailey." He walked into the living room, where she was doing something on her tablet. "What's up?"

"Not much."

"What are you into these days?" God, he sounded horribly uncool.

Bailey didn't say anything.

"Your uncle asked you a question," Angela said.

Bailey sighed. "You know. Stuff."

"Stuff?" Mike said.

"Poisonous frogs and mushrooms," Bailey mumbled.

Had he heard that right? He looked to Angela, who nodded and shrugged.

Well, this was unfortunate.

Mike didn't know anything about frogs and mushrooms, let alone poisonous ones.

He scratched the back of his neck. He was usually pretty good at conversation, but his niece always stumped him.

And then Angela said, "Show him your sketchbook, Bailey."

A sketchbook? Now this sounded interesting.

"You don't have to show me if you don't want to," he said, even though he was intrigued. "If it's private, that's okay." As a child, he'd had zero privacy, and he'd hated it.

"No, you can see." This was a lot of words for Bailey. She reached into a bag, pulled out a hardback black sketchbook, and handed it to him in silence.

He sat down next to her on the couch and flipped through the sketchbook. There were detailed drawings—in pencil crayon—of frogs and mushrooms, the Latin names printed carefully underneath.

The last drawing was of a spider, and Mike instinctively cringed.

He did not like spiders, and this one was, undoubtedly, a poisonous one.

"Have you started drawing poisonous spiders now, too?" Angela asked.

"That spider is venomous," Bailey said. "There's a difference."

"Right. Poisonous is not the same as venomous."

"It's very much *not* the same." Bailey spoke while looking at her tablet.

"There must be poisonous or venomous fish, too," Mike said. "Maybe we could go to the aquarium tomorrow?"

"Okay. Whatever."

That seemed mildly promising. He was glad he'd figured out something for them to do together in the next three days.

But for now…

Mike went to his closet and pulled out a box. At one point, he'd purchased all the art supplies that he hadn't been allowed to have as a kid, but he hadn't used them much.

Watercolors and a fine-tipped black pen. That would work.

He set everything up on the kitchen table, used his phone to do an image search of a poisonous frog Bailey had drawn, and set about copying the picture on his watercolor paper. Eventually, Bailey wandered over and looked at his artwork.

"Cool," she said, much to his delight. "Can I do it, too?"

She hadn't worked much with watercolors before. She was frustrated at first—not that she said so, but he could see it in her expression—but half an hour later, they were quietly painting and drawing poisonous frogs, side by side. Bailey later moved on to spiders, but no fucking way was Mike painting a spider. He stuck with frogs.

It reminded him of when he and Charlotte would draw at her kitchen table. He had fond memories of those days.

The best parts of his childhood.

~

It was the most successful visit with his sister and niece that Mike had ever had. He whistled as he walked to the art supply store on Tuesday afternoon to get some things for Bailey.

True, the reason he'd left the apartment was because Angela had gotten pissed at him. Trying to find something to talk about with Bailey, Mike had mentioned a movie in which a woman poisoned her lover using mushrooms. Now that he thought of it, the movie was probably rated R. He and Angela had subsequently had a minor spat, and he'd decided to get some fresh air.

But really, the last few days—which he'd taken off work so he could spend time with his family—had gone well, and for the first time in a long time, Mike was wondering if he might like to have children.

He had serious doubts about his ability to be a good parent, but surely, he wouldn't be *that* bad, right? He had a very clear idea of what not to do, and he would make every effort to be nothing like his parents.

First, however, he had to get married.

Okay, that wasn't actually a necessity for having a kid, and he knew, from bitter experience, that two parents and two kids with a white picket fence did not mean they were all happy—or anything remotely close to a happy, functioning family. He was positive that Bailey's childhood was better than his and Angela's.

He did like the idea of a long-term relationship, though. Unfortunately, he was thirty-three and it had yet to happen.

Mike was almost at the store when a familiar woman walked out of a coffee shop.

"Hey, Bea!" he said, waving.

She looked at him but didn't wave back. She was wearing sunglasses, so he couldn't properly read her expression.

Did she not remember him? Several years ago, they'd dated for about a month, which was the longest he'd dated anyone.

Or she remembered him as an ass and wanted nothing to do with him.

She's right. You're...

He shoved those thoughts away. They were the reason he'd ended things with her.

He recalled a rather painful "it's not you, it's me" speech that he'd given her while they were in line at Tim Hortons.

It really had been him, not her. He'd only just started therapy and realized he was in no position for a relationship. In fact, he'd been certain he was incapable of love.

But now, he was in a better place, and he had Charlotte. She would teach him. Unlike him, she didn't have a completely messed up family, and she must know something about this stuff, even if had been a while since she'd dated.

Yes, he felt better about his love life now that she was around.

Not that he was interested in Charlotte, even though she was quite attractive. She was still too good for him, but that was okay. They'd help each other, and then he'd go on to meet a woman, and they could have kids who liked poisonous frogs and mushrooms—or possibly kids who had more normal interests. Like baseball. Or crafts.

He was smiling when he returned home with a bag of supplies for Bailey, and the next day, he called Mason.

"I need some advice," Mike said. "I have a date this weekend, and you know restaurants better than I do. What do you recommend?"

"What does she like?" Mason asked sensibly.

Mike scratched his head. "Cider? Vinegar on fries? Too much relish on her hamburgers?"

"That's not terribly helpful."

"Look, I don't know her all that well."

"Yet you know that she likes too much relish on her hamburgers."

Technically, Mike knew that thirteen-year-old Charlotte had liked lots of relish on her burgers. Her tastes may have changed since then, but close enough.

"Wait a second," Mason said. "Is this the childhood friend you met at the bar the other day? She was eating a burger with fries and drinking cider."

"Uh, yeah, might be her," Mike mumbled.

"Do you know where she lives? Which part of the city would be best?"

"Um…"

"There's a new wood-oven pizza place in the Junction," Mason said. "Since you're not giving me much to work with, that's what I'm going to suggest. It's nice, but still pretty casual, and they have a great craft beer and cider list."

Okay, that sounded good.

Mike hoped Charlotte would like it.

[4]

CHARLOTTE MASSAGED her temples and poured more coffee down her throat. Her first practice date with Mike was tonight, but she wasn't feeling the greatest.

Two hours ago, she'd decided to prepare for her date by doing some research. Naturally, she'd Googled "first date horror stories" and looked through pages and pages of results.

There was the woman whose date had insisted on FaceTiming his parents with her, then called her the girl he was going to marry, after they'd spent all of an hour together.

Another woman agreed to let the man pick her up and drive her to the restaurant. Unfortunately, they got rear-ended at a stoplight. Nothing serious, just a scratch, but her date went on a racist, sexist rant and pulled out a sword on the other driver. An actual sword.

The last one Charlotte had read was about a woman whose date spent thirty-seven minutes explaining why Chris Pratt was the best Chris. Thirty-seven minutes!

Why on earth was she interested in dating again?

She'd wanted a guy who was similar to her, who could understand her.

Now it seemed like a miracle if the dude wasn't an asshole who sent unwanted dick pics.

She poured herself more coffee, her hand shaking as she set down the French press. She wasn't sure if she was shaking because of the sheer quantity of caffeine coursing through her veins, or because of all the awful stories she'd read.

It took a lot of coffee to make Charlotte jittery. Caffeine usually just restored her to her normal state—if she went too long without coffee, she got a headache. But five cups in less than two hours was a lot, even for her.

Her phone rang, startling her, and she nearly shrieked.

It was Nicole, asking to be buzzed in.

What was Nicole doing here? Charlotte had a date in an hour and a half and…

Oh, shit.

She now remembered that Nicole had offered to help with her outfit and do her make-up. While frantically reading about nightmarish first dates, Charlotte had forgotten all about that.

There was a knock on the door, and she flung it open.

Nicole tilted her head. "You haven't started getting ready yet?"

Charlotte looked down at her striped pajama pants and tank top. "I should probably shower. I haven't showered in over twenty-four hours."

"Yeah, that might be a good start."

"What are all those bags?" Charlotte gestured to what Nicole was carrying.

"Clothes I bought for you."

"But—"

"Don't worry, I know your size, and I'll return anything you don't like. This is easier than trying to get you to the mall."

Charlotte grimaced at the thought of venturing near a mall.

"You look rather pale," Nicole said. "You okay? Nervous?"

"I just spent two hours reading about what could go wrong on a first date."

Nicole stifled a laugh.

"And now I'm afraid he's going to make me FaceTime his parents," Charlotte said. "Or he'll go on some terrible misogynistic rant or take me to Taco Bell and rave about how it's the best restaurant ever."

"Where *are* you going for dinner?"

"A place in the Junction. Anne's, I think it's called?"

"I've heard of it. It's supposed to be good. See? Nothing to worry about. And you know Mike well enough to be sure he won't FaceTime his parents in the middle of dinner, right?"

"But this isn't all about Mike! It's about the men I might date after him. Besides, I haven't known Mike since grade eight. Maybe he *would* go on a misogynistic rant." Charlotte would be sorely disappointed in him if he did.

Sadly, people could change in ways you didn't want them to.

"I understand your pessimism," Nicole said, "but why didn't you read about good first dates? Ones that led to marriage, for example. Why did you read the horror stories?"

"I wanted to be prepared."

"Alright, alright. Have a shower, then I'll do your hair and we'll pick out an outfit. I thought you could wear your jeans and your brown blazer, but I have a few tops you could wear underneath. Then maybe your ballet flats?"

By the time Charlotte emerged from the shower, she felt a bit calmer. Wearing a bathrobe, she sat on a chair while Nicole blow-dried her hair.

Charlotte rarely used her hairdryer. She was home most of the time, and she just let her hair air-dry. It felt like she was at the hairdresser's now.

Nice to have someone looking after her.

"Let's look at the shirts." Nicole laid them out on Charlotte's couch.

There was a high-cut sleeveless cream-colored shirt, as well as a light pink sleeveless shirt with ruffles. Another pink shirt, this one with short sleeves and a bow at the top. Lastly, a white shirt that would show far too much cleavage for Charlotte's liking. She immediately set it aside.

"Didn't think you'd go for that." Nicole laughed. "But I figured I'd get it, just in case. The cream shirt is rather plain, but wear it with some necklaces, and I think it'll look good."

Charlotte picked up the shirt with the ruffles. Nah, too much. She put it aside.

The bow was a bit much, too, but for some reason, she kind of liked it.

"Can I keep both of these, since I'll hopefully go on a bunch of dates?" Charlotte asked, holding up the two remaining shirts. "I'll send you the money."

"Of course. I'll return the other shirts for you. But maybe you should actually try them on first to be sure you like them."

Charlotte went into her bedroom and came out wearing the cream shirt, blazer, and jeans.

"Now walk like you're on a runway," Nicole said.

Charlotte gave her a death stare.

"I'm kidding," Nicole said. "You look good, though."

"But do I look..." Charlotte hesitated, then whispered the word, "hot?"

Nicole burst into laughter.

"What?" Charlotte said. "I thought I was supposed to look hot when I go on a date."

"I didn't want to make you uncomfortable by saying you look smoking hot."

"You're right. That does make me uncomfortable."

"Now try the other shirt."

Charlotte went back to her bedroom and came out in the pink shirt.

"Work that bow!" Nicole said.

"Stop it."

Nicole laughed again. "You have some teardrop crystal earrings, right? Those would look nice with it."

After Charlotte put on the earrings, Nicole started doing her make-up.

"Nothing too heavy," Charlotte insisted.

"I know, I know, it's not you. I'm just going to give you a smoky eye."

"A light smoky eye."

"And I bought you this." Nicole held up a pink tube of lipstick. "If you don't want it, I'll keep it for myself."

Charlotte wasn't really a lipstick person, but maybe she could try it tonight.

She was going on a date, after all.

She was beginning to feel better. The memory of those dating disaster stories was fading, and she was feeling more confident in her new clothes.

Okay, just a new shirt, but still.

As Nicole worked on her smoky eye, Charlotte started imagining something she hadn't imagined in a very long time.

Walking down the aisle, toward a man who loved her and understood her and—

Ring! Ring!

"Oh my God!" shrieked Charlotte, jumping up. "What on earth is that noise?

"I think it's your phone," Nicole said mildly.

Charlotte grabbed her phone from the other room. It was her sister.

"Hey, Charlotte," Julie said. "I'm downstairs. Can you buzz me up?"

"What's wrong?"

"Nothing's wrong."

"Then why are you stopping by without warning?"

"I have some things to give you. And tell you."

Julie was at her apartment door in no time—she must have

gotten lucky with the elevators—and when she saw Charlotte, she gave her a weird look.

"What's going on with your face?" Julie asked.

"What do you mean?"

Julie steered Charlotte toward the bathroom mirror. She had a single smoky eye…and a weird streak of eye liner on her cheek. Must have happened when she'd jumped up as the phone rang.

"Hey, Julie," Nicole said. "I'm giving Charlotte a light makeover before her date."

"You have a date?" Julie said. "With who?"

Charlotte shrugged. "Not important. Why is it so shocking that I have a date?"

Little sisters could be so freaking annoying.

"If you're not at the cider bar, you spend Saturday nights drinking alone and watching movies."

This was the truth, but Julie made it sound particularly pathetic.

"And you haven't dated in a long time," Julie said. "You mentioned something about swearing off men?"

"I did," Charlotte muttered, "but I decided to give them another chance."

"How exciting!"

"Don't shout in my ear."

"You look…not too bad."

"Such high praise."

"But you know what you should wear? A dress and heels. How long until your date? Since we're the same size, you could wear one of my dresses. I have a sexy black dress that would look great on you. It has a high neckline, don't worry. Of course, it's also backless…"

Charlotte contorted her face in pain.

"You're such a prude," Julie said.

"I'm not." Charlotte just felt more comfortable showing less skin. No judgment on what other people did; it just wasn't her.

"I really think you'd look good in that dress."

"You know I only wear dresses on special occasions."

"But you hate pants, don't you? If you wear a dress, you don't have to wear pants."

Charlotte's little sister had been pissing her off since the day she came out of the womb.

It had been Charlotte's birthday. They'd had a small party, and she'd been about to blow out the candles on the cake when her mom's water broke. Four weeks early.

So, in addition to having her third birthday party interrupted, right before the presents, Charlotte now also shared her birthday with Julie, who'd made her appearance a mere three hours later.

"Pants are better than dresses," she said, "and no fucking way am I wearing heels."

"Yeah, I remember what happened at prom," Julie said. "You—"

"Alright," Nicole said, holding up her hands. "Enough. Charlotte's happy with her current outfit, and this light makeover doesn't involve turning her into someone she's not. Once I get her other eye done, she'll look great for her date with Mike."

"You're going on a date with Mike?" Julie asked.

Damn Nicole.

"There are lots of men named Mike." Charlotte tried to act nonchalant. "It's a common name, so what?"

Unfortunately, she'd never been very good at acting nonchalant.

"It's *Mike* Mike, isn't it?" Julie said.

"I don't know what you mean by Mike Mike."

"Who lived next door when we were kids! He had a crush on you."

"He did not. But yes," Charlotte said sullenly, "it's Mike Guo. We met at the cider bar last weekend."

She didn't say anything about how this was a practice date, not a real date. Julie would make fun of her.

"That reminds me of what I want to tell you," Julie said. "I got a job as a waitress at Ossington Cider Bar. Isn't that cool?"

Are you fucking kidding me?

Charlotte's sister would be invading her refuge outside her apartment. Knowing her luck, Julie would probably always end up working on Saturday nights.

How could this get any worse?

Just then, the phone rang again.

What the hell? Was another person at her apartment?

She looked at the display. It was her parents' landline, and usually she wouldn't be relieved to get a call from her parents, but she was now. No more visitors, thank God.

"Hello," she said.

"Charlotte!" her mother said. "I have not heard from you in a week. What's new?"

"Not much. Same old."

Julie grabbed the phone. "Charlotte has a date tonight."

Charlotte sighed. Things could *always* get worse.

She grabbed the phone back. "Yes, I have a date. No big deal."

"Ah, I am sure he is a great man, knowing you. Good career, very handsome."

"Mm."

"We will meet him the next time we go to Toronto?"

Charlotte choked. "This is a first date. Let's not get too far ahead of ourselves."

Next to her, Julie was laughing, taking far too much amusement in Charlotte's pain.

"Okay," Mom said. "I will let you go and get ready. Make sure to look nice tonight. But don't give him the wrong idea."

Charlotte was about to retort, but her mother had already hung up.

Wow. That had been a short phone call. She wasn't happy with Julie for mentioning the date, but it had gotten her mother off the phone quickly.

She turned around and glared at her sister.

"What?" Julie said innocently. "I didn't tell her it's with Mike. Mom and Dad would have gone crazy had they known."

Nicole shook her head. "I don't get you two."

"You having a sibling, don't you?"

"Yeah, but Cam and I don't bicker and get on each other's nerves this much."

"I think it's mainly Julie getting on my nerves," Charlotte said, "not the other way around. Showing up at my apartment without notice?"

"Ooh, I need to give you your present," Julie said. "I made this one just for you."

Charlotte was rather alarmed. What could it be?

But the necklace Julie held out was lovely. The pendant reminded Charlotte of Spirograph, something she and Mike had loved doing together. The geometric patterns had appealed to her.

"I'm selling them on my Etsy store. What do you think?" Julie's voice held a note of uncertainty, which was unusual.

"It's beautiful, thank you." Charlotte tried to sound sincere rather than sarcastic—something that was tough to do around her sister.

"It doesn't go with what you're wearing today, but you can wear it on a future date with Mike. Spirograph might turn him on." Julie waggled her eyebrows.

What *did* turn Mike on? This was something Charlotte should probably think about.

As Nicole began working on her second smoky eye, Charlotte blurted out, "I need help with being seductive."

This, naturally, reduced Julie to a fit of giggles.

"Don't worry too much about it," Nicole said. "Just be confident. Be yourself."

"Being myself involves wearing pajamas and lazing around the apartment."

"You look good tonight. Lightly touch his arm or leg, unless that makes him uncomfortable. Eye contact. Knowing looks."

What the fuck was a knowing look?

"Bite your lower lip," Julie suggested. "That can be sexy."

"Yeah." Nicole stopped her work on Charlotte's mascara, stood in front of her, tilted her head, and lightly bit her lip.

"Damn," Julie said. "I kinda want to kiss you now."

"Nicole is an expert at this sort of thing," Charlotte said. Her friend might not go on many dates, but she had no shortage of sex.

"Now you try."

Charlotte shook her head. "I'm too, uh, self-conscious to do it now."

"But you'll do it in front of Mike?" Julie batted her eyelashes.

"Shut up."

Julie gasped. "You told me to shut up! I'm telling Mom."

Charlotte rolled her eyes as Julie pulled her phone out of her purse.

"Just kidding," Julie said. "I'll make you some coffee. I bet you want a coffee to perk you up for your date, right?"

"That would be great, thanks." Charlotte may have drunk a lot of coffee this afternoon, but one last coffee for energy and confidence would help.

Julie left the room.

It took Nicole a few more minutes to finish Charlotte's make-up, and when Charlotte looked at herself in the full-length mirror—a gift from her parents—she was impressed with what she saw. Nicole had made her into a sexy version of herself.

Charlotte even wiggled her hips in front of the mirror.

She looked like a woman who was going on a date. A *good* date that did not involve Taco Bell or racist rants.

"Here you go." Julie came into the bedroom with a mug that said *Schist Happens*.

Charlotte looked into the mug. "What the fuck is this? Chamomile tea?"

Julie shrugged. "It's relaxing."

"Chamomile tea isn't relaxing! Do I look relaxed right now?"

"Well, you haven't started drinking it yet."

"I don't like the taste of chamomile," Charlotte said, "and it puts me on edge."

"Why?"

"Because it doesn't have caffeine."

"You're so weird. Don't worry, I was just messing with you."

"Yeah, that's exactly what I needed right now. Thank you."

"I also made coffee," Julie said. "You can give me the tea."

"Where did you get the teabag? It sure wasn't in my cupboard."

"It was in my purse. Lots of interesting things in there."

"Yes, I'm aware. You should clean it out sometime."

Once Charlotte had finished her coffee, which was delivered to her in a *Gneiss Cleavage* mug, and Julie had provided her with more stories of bad first dates—just what she needed—she put on her lipstick and looked at herself in the mirror again.

Yep, she still looked good, if a little anxious.

She left the apartment with Nicole and Julie, who headed to the subway while Charlotte walked north to the Junction.

Man, getting ready for a practice date was bad enough.

How would she ever survive a real date?

[5]

MIKE DRUMMED his fingers on the table, then stopped when he realized what he was doing. No need to be nervous. It was just Charlotte.

Like Charlotte could be "just" anything.

He'd gotten to the restaurant fifteen minutes early, and he'd been seated near the bar. It did have a nice atmosphere, as Mason had promised. Sometimes his friend had questionable taste, such as olive oil ice cream, but he'd done well here. There was lots of wood—exposed beams and such. A little candle flickered at the center of the table.

Mike would have to remember this place for when he was ready to move on to real dating. Although right now, it was hard to think of any woman but Charlotte.

Especially when she was walking across the restaurant, looking totally kick-ass. Like a woman on a mission. Like she was ready to rock this practice date.

He grinned.

He would have pulled out her chair if he thought that was the kind of thing she'd like, but he was pretty sure it wasn't.

Instead, he stood up and gave her a hug.

Charlotte Tam. It was still hard to believe she was back in his life.

He'd missed her, but he didn't say that.

"Did you find the restaurant okay?" he asked.

"Yep, no problem. Just a twenty-minute walk from where I live. Near High Park."

There was a bow on the front of her shirt, just below her throat. It looked so freaking sweet. He wanted to undo it. Not that undoing the bow would expose more of her skin, but he had this intense desire to unwrap her.

As if reading his mind, she took off her blazer.

"It's hot in here, isn't it?" she said.

Oh yeah, it sure was.

The pink shirt had short sleeves—why did he enjoy looking at her arms so much?—and her dark hair fell in soft waves, just to the top of her breasts.

"Why are you looking at me like that?" she demanded, but there was a tremor in her voice. "Is my outfit inappropriate? You're supposed to teach me about dating, so if I'm not wearing the right thing, I want to know. My friend helped me with this—I usually wear old pajama pants all day—but maybe she—"

"You look beautiful, Charlotte. Truly."

"Oh. Thank you." She tucked a lock of hair behind her ear, seeming slightly shy now. She took a sip of water then examined the smudge of pink lipstick on the glass, as if confused by where it had come from.

She probably didn't wear lipstick much, and the fact that she'd done it for him…

Well, his heart beat a little faster.

"Shit," she said. "I probably shouldn't have talked about old pajama pants. Not really a turn-on, right?"

And now he was imagining her in pajama pants and nothing else.

He swallowed. "Don't censor yourself too much. It's fine."

He was about to take a sip of water but then realized she'd taken his water glass. There had only been one glass of water on the table, as he'd been alone when he'd been seated, and the waitress hadn't come around again.

Charlotte realized this a second later. "Shit, I took your water. *Shit*, I'm swearing a lot."

She did seem rather anxious.

Fortunately, he had lots of experience with soothing Anxious Charlotte.

"How about you take a look at the drinks list?" he said, holding it out. "I'm going to order the Honey Blue." He pointed at a cider on the list. A wild blueberry and honey cider from Trash Panda Cidery.

Charlotte made a face.

"What's wrong?" he asked.

"It's listed as semi-sweet. That's too sweet."

"Aw, come on. It's probably not half as sweet as Dr. Pepper." That had been her favorite beverage back in the day. Her parents rarely bought it, but whenever she got to have a soft drink, that was the one she chose.

So many details about Charlotte were coming back to him, and he was learning new ones, too. Like the fact that she hated sweet cider.

"What are you going to get?" he asked.

She scanned the menu, her expression serious. "Get out of my trash."

What? Why was she saying that to him?

Then he looked at the menu and realized it was another cider from Trash Panda Cidery. An oak-aged cider, listed as "dry."

"You sure you want that one and not Roadkill?" he teased. This was a cider aged in wine barrels with raspberries and cranberries.

Was it called "Roadkill" because it was red?

"Tempting, but no," she said. "Maybe later."

He leaned back in his chair, hands behind his head. "What do you have against sweet cider?"

She shuddered.

Charlotte could be very expressive in her movements. Her face didn't hide much, either.

"I don't know," she said. "I just think it tastes better when it's not too sweet. I never liked sweet alcoholic drinks. Coolers?" She made a face. "Ugh."

"Hard lemonade?"

She shuddered again.

For some reason, he enjoyed getting her to do that, and she seemed more relaxed now that she was insulting his taste in cider.

Good. This was exactly what he wanted.

"Cheers, I guess," Charlotte said, holding up her glass.

"You guess?" Mike asked.

His eyes fucking *twinkled*. Who had eyes that actually twinkled?

Mike Guo, apparently.

He grabbed his glass of cider—it was a weird purple color—and tipped it against hers.

"It's been good to see you again," she said honestly.

"Here's to us figuring out dating."

"*Us* figuring out dating? I thought you were supposed to help *me*."

"Right, right. I almost forgot. I'm the lady-killer who's teaching you all about dating."

She snorted before she could try her cider.

And dammit, his eyes were twinkling again.

Yep, he was totally a lady-killer, even if she hated that term. He was wearing a polo shirt and jeans again today, but a different shirt from last time. He had a casual, effortlessly handsome look.

The boy next door.

Why was his smile so damn sexy? Again, it wasn't a calculating sort of sexy. Just easygoing.

They'd always been very different.

"How's your cider?" she asked after he'd tried a sip.

"Very good. Reminds me of blueberry pie."

"A cider should not remind you of blueberry pie. That's wrong."

He passed over his glass and she had a taste.

"Not for me," she said.

He laughed. "Your expression of disgust is priceless."

Yeah, she'd probably been making faces. "Guess I shouldn't do that on a date."

He shrugged. "Can I try yours?"

She slid her glass over, and he tried it and scrunched up his face in an exaggerated fashion, which made her laugh. Then he mimed choking.

"That bad, eh?" she said.

"Not bad at all, but mine's better."

"You have such a sweet tooth."

"What can I say? Guilty."

It was just like talking about nothing in particular with a friend. When Charlotte had gotten to the restaurant, she'd been a little nervous and uncomfortable, but now, she didn't feel too bad.

Though perhaps she should make this a little more date-like.

What had Nicole and Julie suggested she do to be seductive? Something about biting her lip. But was it her bottom or top lip?

This important information had flown out of Charlotte's head. Inconveniently, she still remembered every first-date horror story she'd read this afternoon, although they were no longer at the forefront of her brain.

She was pretty sure it was her top lip, but that seemed rather awkward.

Well, no surprise that seduction came awkwardly to her.

She thrust out her bottom lip and tried to dig her teeth into her top lip. Hmm. That wasn't working right. She tried again.

"What are you doing?" Mike asked. "You're moving your mouth like one of the weird fish I saw at the aquarium on Monday."

An image of Nicole biting her lip suddenly popped into Charlotte's mind. That would have been really helpful ten seconds ago.

Because if Charlotte remembered correctly, Nicole had been biting her lower lip.

"I was, uh, trying to seduce you," she mumbled.

"How was that supposed to seduce me?"

"I was doing it wrong. It was supposed to be like this." Charlotte sank her teeth into her bottom lip, a bit too aggressively. She might be close to drawing blood.

"More like this?" Mike coquettishly bit his lower lip in a way that she hadn't managed. She couldn't help wondering what it would be like if his lips and teeth were on her.

"Dammit, I'm hopeless."

"No, you're not." He leaned forward. "You look very sexy in that outfit."

"Which I didn't pick out myself."

"You drink your dry cider seductively."

"You're not shitting me, are you?"

"I would never. And when you rest your chin in your hand and look at me like I'm a movie star named Chris whose shirt you want to remove, it's sexy, too."

"I do *what*?"

He smiled. "You've done it a couple times. Eye contact is important, and you're doing a good job at it. Don't act so outraged at my compliments."

She tried to speak but couldn't manage to form words.

"Anyway," he said, unbothered by her speechlessness, "I don't think you need the lip-biting trick, but I can teach you, if you like?"

Half an hour later, Charlotte was an expert at biting her lower lip seductively.

Mike sure was good at it. He'd probably had lots of women use this technique on him, and that's why he could do it easily.

She was now on her second cider. Roadkill, which she'd gotten mainly for Mike's amusement, but it was sour and rather tasty. Not as good as Get Out of My Trash! but still pretty good.

Mike had gotten a clementine cider from Prince Edward Cidery, which was far too sweet.

Now, the waitress was setting their pizzas in front of them. Charlotte had ordered one with goat cheese and roasted vegetables; Mike's had cantaloupe, ricotta, and prosciutto, and she did not approve.

Melon on pizza? No, thank you.

She didn't say anything, though, because if she were on a date with a new guy, it probably would be best if she didn't criticize his pizza choices. But if a guy ordered Hawaiian pizza, she might have to say something. She wouldn't be able to help it.

Pineapple on pizza was gross.

And now she remembered that Mike, horror of horrors, had liked Hawaiian pizza when they were kids.

"Want to trade a slice?" Mike asked, after they'd each eaten one of their own.

"Um," she said.

"What's wrong with my pizza? Is it the cantaloupe? You sure have lots of opinions on food and drink."

"Yeah, cantaloupe doesn't belong on pizza."

"Trust me, it's good."

Well, she was a tiny bit curious about how weird it would be, so she relented, and they passed each other a piece of their pizza. Mike took a bite, and her gaze was drawn to his lips.

She'd spent a lot of time looking at his lips tonight. Mostly because he'd been teaching her how to turn someone on by biting her lower lip, of course.

Wait. Had *he* been turned on by watching her bite her lower lip? Not at the beginning, but once she'd mastered it?

Rather than consider that, she tried Mike's pizza. The prosciutto was delicious. The ricotta was delicious. The cantaloupe? Not so much.

"Yours is really good," Mike said, "though not as good as mine."

She narrowed her eyes at him.

"Goat cheese is tasty on pizza," he went on. "Unlike in ice cream."

"You know Treatzz on Ossington? They make an amazing fig goat cheese ice cream. I had it last weekend."

"Oh, is that what you ordered in your bubble waffle?"

How did he—

"I saw you when I was waiting in line." He grinned. "Let me guess. You also ordered the olive oil ice cream?"

"Nope, tiramisu."

"I got lemon meringue and chocolate ginger. Do those meet your approval, unlike my pizza?"

"They're acceptable." Lemon meringue was actually one of her favorites, but she didn't give him the satisfaction of telling him that.

It was easy to be with Mike. She felt like she could relax. Say what she wanted.

They'd always bickered and ribbed each other, but he did it all with a smile on his face, and they'd never had big arguments. Teasing each other about liking Hawaiian pizza or ketchup chips or Dr. Pepper had just been the way they'd interacted. All in good fun.

She hoped she could find a boyfriend who'd talk to her like this.

"So, I was reading about geophysics yesterday," he said. "Tell me a little about what you do, and I'll dazzle you with my knowledge."

"I'm a consultant. People give me data they've had collected, and I interpret it. Sometimes I help them design the surveys, too. I specialize in non-seismic geophysics, mostly magnetics and time-domain EM."

"Damn. I only read about seismics. I'm gonna look stupid now."

"A lot of geophysicists do seismics. But after university, I worked for an airborne company known for its helicopter EM system. It's like…" She grabbed a pen from her purse and drew a helicopter, towing a transmitter and receiver behind it, on a napkin. She started drawing the waveform before realizing this was likely of no interest to Mike and wasn't something she should do on a date. "Anyway." She turned the napkin over. "Airborne surveys can cover a large area, and then I identify areas of further interest, depending on what they're looking for. They might do ground surveys to follow up, then drilling. But mineral exploration can be very boom-bust. When it's bad, there's almost no work. I do some groundwater stuff, too."

"How'd you get into geophysics?"

"There were a few options within geological engineering. I chose geophysics because I was doing well in my physics course." She shrugged. "And I like the idea of using physics to tell you what's underneath the surface. Different deposit types have different properties, so that affects which type of survey is most appropriate."

"I always knew you'd do something cool."

They ate their pizza in companionable silence, and then the waitress came around and asked if they'd like the dessert menu.

"Yes, please." Charlotte could use a coffee, too.

It was a short menu, and it all looked good. She was particularly tempted by the chocolate and coffee mousse, as well as the warm apple ginger crumble with homemade vanilla ice cream. And the tiramisu…

"I'm a little full after the pizza," Mike said. "You want to share something?"

Charlotte almost said, *No, I want my own!*

However, sharing dessert was a very date-like thing to do, right?

"Chocolate coffee mousse or the apple ginger crumble?" she asked.

"Let's do the crumble," he said, "and let's try the ice cider, too."

"It's really, um, expensive. For only two ounces."

"I always wanted to try ice cider. I'll pay, don't worry."

"No. You're doing me a favor by teaching me how to date, therefore I'm paying."

He chuckled. "Alright."

"And I insist you get the ice cider. I'll order one, too."

When the waitress returned, they ordered the apple crumble plus the ice cider, and Charlotte also asked for an espresso.

"I can't believe you drink espresso at eight o'clock at night," Mike said. "That doesn't affect your sleep?"

"I used to drink coffee at all hours, but once I hit thirty, I had to stop drinking it after nine. But I've still got plenty of time before then."

The ice cider from Quebec was indeed amazing. It reminded Charlotte of ice wine, and the process to make it was probably similar. Although it was sweet, that didn't bother her. The rich taste exploded in her mouth. Like dessert in a glass.

They started on their actual dessert, the ice cream melting on the warm spiced crumble. Oh, God. That was incredible. When she moaned in appreciation, she swore Mike's eyes flashed with heat.

She was probably imagining that.

But when she leaned forward to help herself to more crumble, her hand accidentally brushed his, and it did indeed feel like a real date.

When Mike offered to walk her home, Charlotte accepted. It would be better not to walk on the dark streets alone, and this was the sort of thing a date would do, right?

They arrived at her building, and she stopped on the sidewalk.

"You know," she said, "before I left, I spent hours reading first-date horror stories, and that's why I was rather worked up when I arrived."

He laughed softly, and for some reason, this seemed particularly intimate.

"I hope none of them came true," he said.

"No, I had a good time tonight. Thank you. Perhaps this dating business won't be so bad after all." Something suddenly occurred to her. "What am I supposed to do at the end of the night? Are we supposed to kiss?"

"Either of us could make a move, but you shouldn't do anything you don't want to do. If I wanted to kiss a woman, first I'd step closer to her." He did this, and she couldn't help her sharp intake of breath. "Then I'd lean in slightly. If she nodded or leaned forward, I'd kiss her. If it wasn't clear what she wanted, I'd ask. If she stepped back, I definitely wouldn't push it. But some guys are awful, so kick them if they do something you don't like. And if you're ever in a bad situation, call me. I'll come get you no matter what, okay?"

"Thank you." Why did her voice sound so weird and breathy?

"Don't think about what you should do, but what feels right. You don't owe a guy anything, but if you want…" He leaned forward. "Charlotte, would it be okay if I kissed you—"

Oh, God! Yes!

Why did the thought of kissing Mike make her so excited?

"—on the cheek," he finished.

Right. She might ask for actual kissing lessons later, but this was only their first practice date.

"Yes," she whispered.

He cupped her cheek and tilted his head. The press of his mouth on her skin made her want more, but she restrained herself from turning her head so their lips would meet.

Damn, he was good at this. She'd definitely picked the right guy to teach her.

"You want to go out again?" he asked, still standing close to her.

"Yeah. I could use more practice."

"I have something in mind. Would next Saturday afternoon work for you?"

She nodded.

"Okay," he said. "I'll see you."

Once more he pressed his lips to her cheek, and afterward, instead of walking away, he stood on the sidewalk, as though waiting for something. But what?

Perhaps he wanted to make sure she got in the building safely, but her mind was a little mushy after that chaste kiss.

She opened the door, and he waved at her when she was in the lobby. She waved back before going up the elevator, and once inside her unit, she looked at herself in the mirror and attempted to sexily bite her bottom lip.

Not bad.

She wondered what Mike would teach her next time and where they would go.

Who would have thought she'd actually be excited about putting on pants next Saturday and leaving her apartment?

[6]

When he was on the subway the following Saturday, Mike briefly doubted his plan.

He'd chosen something based on what Charlotte had liked as a kid, but it wasn't something that had merely been a passing phase; no, he'd picked an activity she'd enjoyed for all the years he'd lived next to her.

She'd still enjoy it, right? Nostalgia, if nothing else.

He exited the subway at Union and met Charlotte at the street corner, as arranged. He'd told her to dress casually and come prepared for time in the sun. She was wearing jeans and a striped tank top, her hair pulled back in a ponytail, and when he was standing next to her, he could smell sunscreen.

"Is this okay?" she asked. "My outfit, I mean."

"It's perfect."

"When I got here, I started worrying that when you said 'casual,' you meant something fancier than what I consider casual, and…"

He should be paying attention to what she was saying, but he was hopelessly distracted by her shoulders, of all things. And the fact that this tank top was a little lower cut than what she'd worn last weekend.

He nearly reached for her hand but then stopped. Hand-holding seemed a bit serious for a second date, right?

"Where are we going?" she asked.

"It's a secret," he said.

She rolled her eyes.

"Don't worry. You'll find out soon enough."

They headed west, and ten minutes later, they were nearly at their destination, along with thousands of other fans, some wearing Blue Jays hats and jerseys.

"You're taking me to the SkyDome," she said.

"What is this, nineteen ninety-nine? It's the Rogers Centre."

She glared at him, but the glare seemed half-hearted. Missing her usual spunk.

Why wasn't she glaring more enthusiastically? And why was he so obsessed with getting under her skin?

"Anything wrong?" he asked. "I figured a ballgame would be a nice casual date, and you always liked the Jays."

"Very true."

Something still wasn't right, but he couldn't figure it out.

Instead, he squeezed her hand, and they headed into the stadium together.

Charlotte admitted this was a reasonable place for a date, if Mike was under the impression she liked baseball and the Jays. Which he was.

But since Brad's failed proposal, she'd lost interest.

It seemed silly to mention that, so she kept quiet as Mike led her to their seats. They weren't in the nosebleeds, but they weren't super close to the action, either.

Good. She was glad he hadn't spent too much money on this.

Mike got them each a beer, and they chatted a bit about the Blue Jays of their youth. They'd occasionally watched games together at her house. He'd liked Roberto Alomar; she'd preferred John Olerud.

But once the game started, Charlotte began to feel more uneasy. She couldn't help remembering. Those words on the scoreboard. Her initial conviction that they were for someone else, and then her dawning horror as she realized otherwise.

Brad on his knees. Her desperate escape.

Running, running, running…

"What's wrong?" Mike asked in the bottom of the second.

She said nothing.

"We can leave if you'd like. I thought this was something you'd enjoy, but I was basing that on my knowledge of thirteen-year-old Charlotte Tam."

"It's stupid," she muttered.

"I'm sure it's not stupid."

For some reason, as she looked into his eyes, she was overcome with the urge to tell him.

"My ex proposed here," she said.

Mike's easy smile disappeared. "At a Jays game?"

"Yes."

"You said no?"

"Correct." She hesitated. "A scoreboard proposal was literally my worst nightmare."

"I remember. I was there the first time you witnessed one on TV."

And she now recalled that Mike had drawn her a picture of John Olerud to make her feel better after her proposal-slash-scary-monster dream in grade two.

"Brad knew," she said, "but—"

"What was he thinking?" Mike shook his head. "Even if I hadn't witnessed the horror on your face when you saw that proposal, I'd know you'd never want to get engaged like that. Too many people. Too much attention."

At least that was obvious to someone.

"It's even worse when you can't say yes," she said. "People were shouting at me, telling me not to break his heart, and I just ran. I got the fuck out of the stadium as fast as possible and officially broke up with him on the phone. There were videos of me running away on social media."

"I'm sorry, Charlotte."

Mike rubbed his hand in circles over her shoulder. A friendly gesture, she told herself.

"I probably shouldn't tell that story on a second date," she said.

"I'm glad you told me."

"Would you ever propose like that at a baseball game?"

"Nah."

"Really?" she said.

"Why is that so surprising?"

"I don't know. You're a lot different from me. More like Brad."

"I'm insulted you're comparing me to that man."

She chuckled. "Have you ever proposed?"

"No."

How many ex-girlfriends did Mike have? She couldn't help wondering.

"But when I do," he said, "it'll be private. Just the two of us. Maybe somewhere in nature. After you saw the scoreboard proposal on TV, I remember you said it wasn't romantic at all."

"I only had a fuzzy idea of what romance was back then, but yeah."

"You said you wanted a field of flowers with *nobody* watching. I think you were on to something. That could be nice, or surrounded by red and golden maple leaves in the autumn."

She pictured Mike down on one knee, staring lovingly up at someone. She was jealous of this imaginary woman.

Silly of her.

"We can go," Mike said. "I understand if you don't want to be here."

"No, I don't want to continue to let Brad ruin baseball for me. Fuck him. We're going to stay, and I'm going to enjoy myself." She chugged half her beer. "Have you been to any baseball games recently?"

"I go with friends maybe once a year, and last year I took my niece."

"You have a niece?"

"Her name is Bailey, and she's ten."

"Wow. It's hard to imagine Angela having a ten-year-old. She wasn't much older than ten the last time I saw her. Bailey likes baseball?"

"No, I quickly discovered she hates it. I was just hoping to find something we might enjoy together. Now she's into poisonous frogs and mushrooms."

"You're joking."

"Nope. It's cool that there's finally something we both enjoy."

"Um…"

"She likes drawing them, and I got her into watercolors the last time she visited. What about Julie? How's she doing?"

"She's in Toronto. We don't see each other a lot—you know how we were never close. She just got a job at Ossington Cider Bar, and she makes jewelry on the side. She made this, actually." Charlotte lifted up the pendant on her necklace.

"Reminds me of Spirograph," Mike said. "I loved Spirograph."

"Me, too."

Just then, the stadium erupted in cheers. One of the Jays had hit a homerun, but Charlotte had missed it because she'd been engrossed in her conversation with Mike. She didn't cheer, but she smiled as she sipped her barely-cold beer.

This was kind of nice. She was glad he'd taken her here.

She bought them hotdogs in the fourth inning, but after that, she kept her eyes on the field—and occasionally on Mike. Even when she wasn't looking at him or talking to him, she appreciated his presence.

At the seventh-inning stretch, however, something unexpected happened.

Though perhaps Charlotte shouldn't say it was unexpected. Given her luck, it was exactly the sort of thing that would happen to her.

TAMARA KIRK, I LOVE YOU. WILL YOU MARRY ME?

The words appeared on the jumbo screen, followed by a shot of a man getting down on one knee in front of a woman, both of them wearing Jays jerseys.

"Oh God, oh God," Charlotte muttered.

She tensed as she imagined herself in the woman's position, and Mike squeezed her hand.

But then the couple was kissing and people were cheering, and she breathed out a sigh of relief, glad it had worked out better for them than it had for her.

In fact, she started laughing.

Her first baseball game in five years and she'd witnessed a proposal.

"You okay?" Mike asked.

"Yeah." She laughed again. "I'm just fine."

The concern disappeared from his face, but he didn't let go of her hand. Nor did he say something inane like, *See, baseball game proposals aren't so bad after all.* He understood they weren't for her and never would be.

See, Charlotte, not all men are terrible.

Brad—and the excessive number of dating horror stories she'd read—may have given her a skewed perspective.

For the first time in a long time, she felt hope. Real hope.

She *could* find a decent man who understood her, and maybe that man didn't need to hate wearing pants and leaving the apartment as much as she did. Just because he was different from

Charlotte didn't mean he'd think there was something wrong with her or want to change her.

Well, that widened her dating pool quite a bit.

She turned her attention back to the game. The Jays were down by three runs to the Orioles, but after a couple runs in the eighth inning, followed by a homer in the bottom of the ninth, the Jays tied it up and the game went to extra innings.

When the Jays' second baseman hit a double in the eleventh inning, sending a runner home, Charlotte actually cheered out loud.

"So," Mike said, "your return to baseball was a success?"

"It was. Thank you."

And then she leaned in and gave him a fleeting kiss on the cheek.

~

The taco joint erupted in cheers.

Mike had been in the middle of teasing Charlotte for ordering three tacos al pastor rather than ordering three different types. Personally, he preferred variety.

But he trailed off and looked to the back of the restaurant, just in time to see a man stand up—he'd been down on one knee—and throw his arms around another man. They kissed.

"Did we just witness another proposal?" Mike asked.

"We sure did." Charlotte didn't seem at all bothered by this. "The blond guy said something about how he fell in love on their very first date, which was at this restaurant. You didn't hear?"

"No, I was too busy insulting your choice in tacos."

She gave him a look.

"Aw, Charlotte," he said. "You think it's sweet, don't you?"

"Well, returning to the site of your first date is rather sweet, yes. But if someone did that for me, I'd hope they'd book the whole restaurant or arrange a private room."

Mike found himself wondering if Anne's had any private rooms or—

What on earth was he thinking? This was only their second date, and he was supposed to be teaching Charlotte about dating.

Teaching, not actually dating her.

And secretly teaching himself while pretending that he was some kind of lady-killer with lots of knowledge in this department.

But as he looked across the table at her, digging into her taco with gusto—why did she approve of pineapple on tacos but not on pizza?—he felt a certain fondness in his chest that he didn't normally feel for a friend.

He'd loved her, before they'd been old enough to even drive or vote, and some of that was returning.

Though it was different now.

She picked up a piece of pineapple that had fallen out of her taco and slid it between her lips. He tried not to laugh at the thought of the seductive lip-biting lessons he'd given her last weekend.

God, she was adorable, and she would almost certainly scowl if he told her that.

Which was even more adorable.

Something about the baseball game, the way she'd told him about Brad—what was it about seeing a vulnerable side of Charlotte that brought out his feelings for her?

He didn't know.

"Dammit, I'm getting a headache," Charlotte said as she polished off her final taco.

He paused in eating, nearly finished his bulgogi taco. "Do you need a painkiller? I don't have one, but—"

"No, it's caffeine withdrawal. Thirteen-year-old Charlotte had yet to be introduced to the wonders of coffee, but thirty-two-year-old Charlotte is a coffee addict."

"Thirty-two-year-old Charlotte talks about herself in the third person. Good to know."

She stuck out her tongue at him, then said, "Probably not a turn-on to have me stick out my tongue and complain about my caffeine-withdrawal headache. I shouldn't do that on a date."

He was just glad she was comfortable with him. They hadn't seen each other for twenty years, but it was easy to hang out with her again.

"I haven't had any coffee since this morning," she said. "Hard to believe I went eight hours without thinking about coffee."

"Must have something to do with my scintillating company."

"Yeah, I'm sure that's it," she said sarcastically, but then she smiled at him. "Your scintillating company, that exciting baseball game, and two proposals."

"I'll be finished in a minute, and then we can leave. Chris's Coffee Shop is two minutes from here." He'd do whatever it took to keep her supplied with coffee.

"Excellent."

It had turned out to be a good day, despite Charlotte's initial discomfort with watching a ballgame, and he had an idea for their next date. Something else related to their childhood, but a grown-up version. Hopefully she'd like it.

Mike had only ever wanted to make her happy.

[7]

Charlotte walked through the cider bar, her gaze darting around as she looked for her sister. Fortunately, it appeared Julie wasn't working tonight.

Breathing out a sigh of relief, Charlotte took a seat at her friends' table on the patio. Sierra and Amy were already there.

"Hey!" Amy said. "I haven't seen you in a while. I can't believe I couldn't come last time. Sounds like it was exciting!"

"Yeah, I guess it was exciting," Charlotte said mildly.

The table next to them was loud. Dammit. She might get a headache that had nothing to do with caffeine withdrawal.

"So, how were your practice dates?" Nicole asked, sliding into the seat beside Charlotte. "You told me you went on two, but you didn't give any details. And I want *details*."

"Dinner was fine, and then we went to a baseball game last weekend." Charlotte shrugged, but she expected her friends wouldn't be as calm.

"He took you to a *baseball game*?" Sierra's loud voice rivaled the volume of the table next to theirs. "You haven't been to the Roger's Centre since—"

"That's right. But it turned out okay. I enjoyed myself."

Sierra, Nicole, and Amy all gave her skeptical looks.

Luckily, the server came around to take their orders, but as soon as he was gone, Nicole said, "You enjoyed yourself? You weren't thinking about Brad?"

"Oh, I was. But I told Mike about it, and then, I dunno, it was okay. We even witnessed a proposal at the game. Unlike me, she said yes." Charlotte chuckled at the memory.

"I think she likes him, don't you?" Sierra turned to Nicole.

"Yeah, I think so," Nicole said.

"No," Charlotte protested. "I don't like him…that way. He's my friend. Sure, he's attractive, but—"

"I think you do like him that way," Amy said.

"And you actually told him about Brad and had a good time at a Jays game," Sierra said. "That has to mean something."

Charlotte shook her head. "I assure you, it means nothing. Except that we're friends."

"And you think he's super sexy and want to sleep with him," Nicole added.

"I said no such a thing."

"It's in your facial expression."

Charlotte schooled her face into a scowl.

"You should date him for real," Sierra said. "As I told you last time. None of this practice date nonsense."

"But he's helping me with dating," Charlotte said. "He really is. It's good for me to be comfortable spending time one-on-one with a guy. I'm feeling much better about the prospect of dating now. I've discovered that not all men are colossal jerks, but I'm not interested in him, I promise. He's a good teacher."

"Mm-hmm." Nicole still sounded skeptical. "What has he taught you?"

"How to sexily bite my bottom lip, for example."

"Julie and I were the ones who taught you that."

"But I didn't practice with you, and when I went to try it with Mike, I bit my top lip instead."

Nicole burst into laughter. "And then he set you straight?"

"Yeah, he spent a while teaching me how to do it properly."

"You didn't need Mike for that. I could have provided further assistance if you'd asked."

"I bet he enjoyed watching you bite your lower lip," Sierra said. "It probably turned him on, and that's why he was happy to practice."

Nicole nodded. "Did he give you kissing lessons, too, Charlotte?"

Charlotte hesitated. "No."

"Mm-hmm."

"No, really! He didn't. He just kissed me on the cheek after our first date."

"And by 'kissed me on the cheek,' you mean, 'stuck his tongue down my throat'?"

Charlotte attempted her best death glare.

"Sorry," Nicole said. "You're too much fun to tease. I'll stop, but it does seem as if you like him, and I always thought this plan to practice dating was foolish."

"Where's Rose?" Sierra asked. "She's not here to defend her idea. Not that she thought Charlotte should go on practice dates with Mike, but the love lessons were her suggestion."

"Rose is on holiday with her family for the long weekend, remember?"

Their ciders arrived, and Charlotte contemplated going on holiday with her own family...and immediately drank a third of her cider.

She hadn't particularly enjoyed family vacations as a kid. Her parents had insisted on cross-country road trips so they could see as much of Canada as possible, but Canada was a freaking enormous country, and being trapped in a car for days with her parents and little sister had not been her idea of fun.

And now? It would only be worse.

"I can't imagine going on vacation with my family," Sierra

said, voicing Charlotte's thoughts. "My parents would spend the entire twelve-hour car ride or plane trip critiquing my life choices, from my job to my clothes."

"Cam and I travel together," Nicole said, "but with our parents, it would be weird. They wouldn't enjoy having us around anyway, since they like to be able to make out whenever they want. But it's different for Rose."

They all nodded and were silent for a moment.

"Anyway," Sierra said, turning to Charlotte, "when are you and Mike going on your next 'practice' date?" She used air quotes around "practice," which Charlotte decided to ignore.

"Tomorrow."

"Where are you going?" Amy asked. "If you need ideas for dates, I have tons."

"He has something in mind," Charlotte said.

"He's putting a lot of effort into these practice dates," Sierra said. "Very interesting."

Charlotte threw up her arms in exasperation. "Can we talk about something other than my practice boyfriend?"

"Now he's your practice boyfriend, not just your practice date?"

"Did he like the outfit I picked out for you?" Nicole asked.

"I asked him if it was acceptable," Charlotte said, "and he said yes."

"I'm sure 'acceptable' was the word he used."

He'd said "beautiful," something she doubted she'd forget, but she wasn't giving her friends any more ammunition.

"Alright," Amy said, "I've got a question to ask you all about my wedding favors."

Amy pulled out her phone, and Charlotte shot her a grateful look.

Her friends hadn't gotten to tease her about men for many years, and it appeared they were making up for lost time, just because she was dipping her toe back into the dating game.

She hated to think of how much they'd tease her when she went on a *real* date.

~

"How was your date the other week?" Mason asked. "Did she like Anne's?"

"Yeah." Mike took a sip of his beer. "It was a good spot for a first date. Thanks for the rec, by the way."

It was the Saturday of the August long weekend, and he and Mason were at a bar in the west end. Drinking beer, talking about nothing in particular. There was a baseball game on the TV above the bar, and it made Mike think of Charlotte.

"She objected when I ordered semi-sweet cider. And pizza with cantaloupe on it."

"Pizza with cantaloupe, eh?" Mason said.

"And prosciutto and ricotta cheese."

"That does sound good. Maybe I'll make some tomorrow. Got nothing else to do, and I always wanted to try making pizza dough from scratch."

Mike shook his head. "Why? It's so easy to buy pizza. You don't have to fiddle with yeast."

"I don't understand why people are so scared of yeast."

"I'm not afraid of it. Just don't see the point in using it myself. Like I don't see the point of this." Mike flicked Mason's toque.

Mason laughed. "Don't you dare insult my toque."

"I'll stop with the insults when it's November, I promise."

"So, you like this woman, even if she doesn't approve of fruit on pizza."

"Yeah, it's going well."

Mike wasn't going to tell Mason the truth about Charlotte and how she wanted dating lessons. He didn't want to seem too weird.

"You got another date lined up?" Mason asked.

"Tomorrow night." Mike paused. "Cody's up at the cottage with his parents for the long weekend. Why are you in the city?"

"To hang out with you and make pizza from scratch, what else? But seriously, my parents are in Europe right now, so I can't go to Guelph to visit them, and the weather's not supposed to be nice for the rest of the weekend anyway."

Mason didn't ask about Mike's family. He might wear toques in the peak of summer and have questionable taste in ice cream—and seriously, who had questionable taste in *ice cream?*—but he was a good guy who didn't try to push Mike's boundaries.

A few years ago, Mike had told his friend a little about his past. *I had a fucked-up childhood and needed to spend years in therapy. I no longer talk to my parents because all they do is make me feel bad about myself.*

Mike wasn't interested in sharing more than that.

No, he'd rather talk sports and food. He had a good life now, and his past didn't affect him much anymore.

Aside from the fact that you've never really had a girlfriend.

Mike looked up at TV and remembered how hard Charlotte had laughed when they'd witnessed that proposal at the ballgame.

Tomorrow. He would get to see her again tomorrow. At Nautilus.

$$[\ 8\ ]$$

"Wow," Charlotte said.

Mike smiled, pleased with her reaction. "You liked Jules Verne books when we were little, so I figured you might appreciate a steampunk bar."

"It's called Nautilus after the submarine in *Twenty Thousand Leagues Under the Sea?*"

"I think that's the reason for the name, yes."

"It's been so long since I've read those books. But I do read steampunk, among other things."

She stood on her toes in the middle of the hot-air balloon room and kissed him. On the cheek, but still. It was damn nice to have her lips on his skin, her body pressed against his in the small room.

"Brad never took me anywhere like this," she said, and he felt a stupid amount of pride.

"I don't know what he was thinking." Mike shook his head. "Third date, steampunk bar. Everybody knows this."

She laughed as she turned her attention to the dozens of small hot air balloons hanging from the ceiling. There was a mural on the wall, depicting a man in the basket of a hot air balloon.

"I can't believe I've never heard of this place," Charlotte said. "My friends live in the Annex, just a ten-minute walk from here."

The bar was in a sprawling—well, what would be considered sprawling in downtown Toronto—Victorian house just off Bloor. There were lots of rooms, each slightly different.

The next room had a large blimp suspended from the ceiling. Ropes hanging from the blimp were attached to a basket, which was a cozy seating area for two people. A man and a woman were currently occupying it, much to Mike's disappointment. He'd very much like to sit there with Charlotte, their knees bumping together.

Her gaze, however, was on the bar, which had an intricate design of interlocking gears.

Or perhaps she was looking at the mustached bartender, who was wearing a collared shirt, tie, waistcoat, cape, and top hat with gears on it.

"Tonight's lesson," Mike murmured to Charlotte. "Don't check out other men when you're on a date."

She graced him with a scowl. "I was not checking him out."

"No? Then what were you doing?"

"Trying to figure out how you'd look in that outfit."

"Oh, really. Do you think I could pull it off?"

She studied him for a moment that seemed to stretch on and on. He could look nowhere but at Charlotte, though he heard clanks and hisses in the background, as well as soft conversation from other patrons.

Mike struck a pose under Charlotte's watchful eye and pretended to twirl his non-existent mustache, then checked his imaginary pocket watch.

"Tsk, tsk, you're taking a long time to answer," he said.

Charlotte glared but continued to study him. "I think you could do it, though I'm not sure the cape is your style."

"But the top hat and everything else are my style?"

She shrugged. "It would be kind of hot, actually."

"Charlotte Tam, are you blushing?"

"Shut your mouth." She led him to another room. "Or this kraken will attack you."

The next room was, indeed, dominated by a large metal kraken, attacking a wooden ship—this, too, was a small seating area, and it was also currently occupied. There were high-top tables scattered throughout the room. Most people were dressed in normal clothes, but one woman was wearing what looked like a steampunk adventurer's costume.

"Do you want to grab a table?" Mike asked.

"No," Charlotte said, "I want to see the rest of this place."

She grabbed his hand and pulled him into the next room. This one was less exciting than the others, but it had heavy velvet drapes, pulled back and tied with gold rope, revealing what was supposed to be the view out a window—except it was a mural, showing an exciting world with airships.

Mike was admiring the skill of the artist, but then Charlotte pulled him up the narrow, creaky staircase, and he'd follow her wherever she went.

And he loved seeing her flushed and excited about something. It was rare.

The first room upstairs was a sort of science lab, with two "scientists" behind the bar. One man and one woman, busy mixing drinks.

"Would I look good in one of those outfits?" Mike whispered to Charlotte. "Do those goggles turn you on?"

"Oh, fuck off."

He was pretty sure she meant that affectionately.

And, miracle of miracles, she was still holding his hand.

A waitress walked by, wearing a brown corset and a long black skirt. A hat was precariously tilted on her head.

"Would you wear that?" he asked, leaning down to whisper in Charlotte's ear. "I think you'd look hot in a corset."

And nothing else.

"You'd like that wouldn't you?" She dropped his hand and trailed her fingers up his arm. He hissed out a breath.

And then she stepped away from him.

"Mike," she said, "what are we doing?"

"We're flirting. Practice, you know. For your dates."

"But you didn't tell me we were practice flirting. It seemed natural."

"You tend to overthink things. I figured it was better not to tell you what I was doing."

He was talking out of his ass, of course.

Practice? Ha.

He simply wanted to flirt with her.

"It's easy with you." Charlotte sounded puzzled. "Flirting, I mean. Is flirting always this easy, and I've been overthinking it all these years?"

He didn't know how to answer that.

Just then, there was a very loud crash in the background music, and Charlotte jumped toward him and gripped his shoulder.

"What the fuck," she murmured. "They should warn people about that."

Unlike the clanking-and-hissing soundtrack downstairs, the ominous music upstairs made Mike feel like he was in a movie.

He bowed over her hand. "Lady Charlotte, will you do me the honor of this dance?" he asked, knowing full well she'd be outraged by the idea.

"In your dreams, pal," she said. "And this isn't dance music. It's the-kraken-is-about-to-attack music."

He stepped back and forth, swaying his hips as he snapped his fingers. "Anything is dance music if you feel like it."

"I do not feel like it."

"It could be good practice for a date."

She considered this for a split second before saying, "If he expects me to go dancing with him, he can fuck right off." She crossed her arms over her chest.

"Good to know, good to know." Mike kept dancing. A few people were looking at him, but he didn't care. He didn't mind making a slight fool of himself, especially when Charlotte's lips were twitching. "I guess I'll have to pull out all my moves to convince you."

He started doing the Macarena, which had been popular during their childhood, much to Charlotte's distress.

That got the biggest laugh out of her yet, so it was totally worth it.

He was about to suggest they move to the next room, but then fog starting emanating from a machine in the corner, and when would he ever get to do the Macarena in the fog again, while the-kraken-is-about-to-attack music played in the background?

"You're a nut," Charlotte whispered, laughing.

He took a bow. A couple women clapped.

They headed to another room, which was filled with more gears on the walls than Mike had ever seen in his life before.

"I wonder what's in here," Charlotte said, pushing aside a curtain.

As soon as he saw, he swallowed hard.

There were lots more gears on the walls, but right behind the curtain was a sofa of sorts. He thought this was called a chaise longue, but he wasn't sure.

"Excellent," she said. "Nice and private."

Yep, he could think of a whole bunch of things he'd like to do with Charlotte here, but that probably wasn't what she had on her mind. She tended to seek out solitude when she was in a busy place, that was all.

But then she said, "It's the perfect place for our kissing lessons."

"*Kissing lessons?*" he sputtered.

~

"I haven't kissed a guy in five years," Charlotte said. "I'm woefully out of practice."

Mike was staring at her, uncharacteristically silent.

"Isn't the third date when things often get physical?" she continued. "I can't remember whether that's kissing or sex, though. I read all sorts of advice columns this week, and now I'm terribly confused. But I think kissing…"

Oh, God, she was babbling. Charlotte *never* babbled.

And Mike still wasn't speaking.

"Of course," she said, "if you're not comfortable with kissing lessons, we don't have to, but I'd appreciate the help."

This room wasn't big enough to contain all the tension.

"Yeah, sure, we can kiss," he said at last, sounding all casual.

She was more excited about these lessons than she ought to be.

"Do you have any tips for me?" she asked.

He scratched the back of his head. "It's hard to give tips for kissing, especially when…"

Especially when what? The thought that maybe he didn't actually have much kissing experience popped into her head, but she pushed it aside.

"Don't go overboard on using your tongue," he said at last.

She nodded. This much she knew. Before Brad, she'd briefly dated someone who'd used too much tongue when they kissed, and it had seemed like he was trying to do tongue acrobatics.

It was good to be reminded of such things so she didn't do them herself.

"What else?" she asked.

"Just find the right moment," he said. "And live in the moment. Don't think about when you'll get your next cup of coffee—"

"Hey! I'd never think of that during a kiss. But 'live in the moment'? That's cheesy."

He shrugged. "Like I said, it's difficult to give kissing advice. A lot of it is the timing, the person."

Yeah, that was likely true.

Still, Charlotte wanted practice with someone she wasn't actually dating. It wouldn't be the perfect kiss, but it would get her used to the idea of kissing someone again and...

Whoa. Mike was leaning toward her. Were his eyes always that dark, dark liquid brown? He lifted his hand, and his fingertips grazed her skin before he settled them on her cheek.

She actually moaned.

It had been a long time since she'd been touched like this, that was all, and Mike knew what he was doing.

He leaned closer, and she started breathing quickly in anticipation.

He brushed his lips, ever so lightly, over hers, and when she cupped the back of his neck, he kissed the corner of her lips, then down her jaw, to a very sensitive place at the top of her neck—how did he knew about this spot? *She* hadn't even known.

"Mike," she breathed.

His lips were on hers now, coaxing them open. In her shock, it took her a moment to respond.

But then, it was the most natural thing in the world. The play of her lips against his. Sliding her hand under the hem of his shirt so she could touch warm skin. He placed one hand on her lower back and brought her closer as he swept his tongue into her mouth.

He muttered something under his breath, and she was about to ask if he was okay, but then he sat down and pulled her into his lap. She cupped both of his cheeks in her hands and kissed him eagerly, wanting to taste as much of him as she could. More, more, more.

God, it felt good. Why had it been so long since she'd kissed someone?

Her skin prickled everywhere, and she clenched her thighs and…

Oh.

His erection.

She wanted to take off her jeans, and not simply because she hated wearing proper pants, but because she wanted to be closer to Mike. She pictured him on top of her, sliding into her.

He growled in the back of his throat, and it was thrilling.

"Charlotte," he murmured, kissing her jaw.

Then he lifted her off him, and she nearly sobbed at the loss of contact.

In the distance, there was ominous music, and she recalled that they were in a steampunk bar. They hadn't even had a drink yet. They were behind a curtain, where a lot of people had probably made out over the years.

Including her.

"Sorry, I got carried away," he said, not meeting her eyes.

"Don't be sorry. I liked it."

As she watched his smile grow, her heart was *thump, thump, thumping* in her chest.

"I didn't know a kiss could be like that," she surprised herself by saying. "You're certainly good. You must have had lots of practice."

"Practice kiss," he muttered. "Right."

He was behaving oddly.

Clearly, she hadn't dated guys who were very good at kissing. It was exciting to know it could be different from her past experiences. What would her first *real* kiss in five years be like?

"Are all of your kisses like this?" she asked.

She expected a slightly cocky *yeah* in response.

"No," he said softly, and something skittered through her body.

Huh. Maybe *she* was unusually good at this kissing business.

Then his expression changed, as if their instructional kiss hadn't happened.

"Shall we get a drink?" he asked, smiling.

How could he smile like that now? As though he hadn't just suggested that kisses with her were special?

And he'd brought her to this unique bar because he thought she'd love it. If this was what dating someone who actually understood her was like, she wanted more.

But then he said, "I have some homework for you."

Homework?

He curled his hand around her waist. "I want you to kiss me again—"

She immediately put her lips to his.

He stood up and laughed. "Not now. Sometime later tonight, when the moment is right."

Well, she was definitely looking forward to this homework.

The problem was that Charlotte didn't want to do her homework just once.

After their initial practice kiss, they went to the science lab bar, and she got a kraken martini. The stem of the glass was a tentacle. The martini was quite dry, and she approved.

Mike got some kind of fruity cocktail, and for some reason, she wanted to taste it on his lips. When they were standing outside on one of the house's many balconies, she leaned in and kissed him and nearly lost her grip on her tentacle martini glass.

It had only been ten minutes, but she'd forgotten just how amazing it felt.

They stayed on the balcony, sipping their cocktails, for a few minutes. It was a small balcony with no seating, and no room for anyone but them.

After she'd finished her drink, she looked at her watch. It was almost nine, and it had been far too long since she'd had coffee.

She worried her bottom lip between her teeth—not in a sexy way this time.

"What's up?" Mike asked.

"I want coffee."

"I thought you might."

He led her inside and up another flight of stairs. The ceiling was low, the roof sloping, and the third floor looked a bit like what she imagined a Victorian tea salon would be like. It was brighter than the rest of the bar, and there was an intricate steampunk-themed coffee machine on the counter.

She couldn't help it: she kissed Mike again, even though there were other people in the room who could witness their kiss.

Weirdly, she didn't care.

In addition to tea sandwiches, scones, pots of tea, and cups of coffee, the little café also served boozy coffee and tea cocktails.

Coffee and alcohol together? Sounded good to Charlotte.

After they finished their beverages, they returned to the second floor. The fog machine was working its magic in the science lab, and didn't every woman dream of being kissed in the fog?

She kissed Mike once more, feeling brave enough to use tongue this time, but she was careful not to overdo it, remembering his advice.

But then his advice flew out of her mind, and she just kept kissing him.

Down on the first floor, the seats in the blimp basket were empty, and Mike suggested they claim it before anyone else did. She sat down and watched as he went up to the bar and ordered drinks from the man in the top hat.

She bet the bartender wasn't as good of a kisser as Mike. She hadn't known how Mike could kiss when they'd been down here earlier, but now she did, and she was a changed woman.

He came back with their drinks and they sat side by side, his thigh pressing against hers. She gave him another kiss, because how often would she get to kiss someone in the basket of a blimp?

At the end of the night, he walked her home from High Park subway station. And at the entrance to her building, she kissed him again.

She wound her arms around his neck, and he put his hands on her waist, and they kissed in the light of the entryway. Although she'd kissed him quite a bit tonight, it definitely wasn't getting old, and her body hadn't stopped responding. He held her against him as though he wanted her as close as possible. Yes, he sure knew how to make a woman feel wanted.

She stepped back as the reality of their situation washed over her. They were practice dating and practice kissing, yet for much of the evening, it had felt *real*.

"How did I do on my homework?" she asked.

Because that's what those kisses had been. Homework.

"A-plus," he said without hesitation. "You went above and beyond."

"That's good to hear. I always aim for perfection."

He treated her to a lopsided smile before walking away.

She couldn't manage to open the door to the building. She just stood there, stunned by the events of the evening.

What if she dated Mike? Actually dated him, not as any kind of lesson.

The fact that tonight had been so good...perhaps it meant something, other than that he understood her and was a skilled kisser.

Nah, this was Mike Guo, and he was simply the right person to ease her back into the idea of dating and give her some practice, that was all.

Satisfied, she stepped into the building, ignoring the doubts at the back of her brain, the ones telling her that this could be more than practice.

[9]

MIKE DECIDED to walk home from Charlotte's. It was a nice night, and he lived about a forty-five-minute walk from her apartment. He hadn't told her that he lived so close. Twenty years later, and they were living only four kilometers apart. How about that?

Twenty years later, and he still had feelings for her.

Or had feelings for her again.

Which was more accurate?

He touched two fingers to his lips, lips which had kissed her over and over tonight. She'd certainly seemed to enjoy kissing him. The quiet sounds she made, and the one time she'd practically bucked against him…

She'd initiated many kisses over the course of the night, then asked him how she'd done on her homework.

That had snapped him back to reality.

But it was possible she'd changed her mind and wanted this to be real, wasn't it?

It had to be possible.

Mike couldn't bear to shatter his own dreams. Tonight had been a glimpse of what it would be like to be with her, really be with her, and it hadn't let him down.

His yearning almost scared him.

But Charlotte had been special from the very beginning, from the day he'd asked if he could draw on the driveway with her.

For years, he'd been too much of a mess for a relationship, even if outwardly it wasn't obvious. Then he'd sorted himself out, more or less, but he'd still been a little frightened about getting close to someone.

Maybe it would be easier with Charlotte, who'd known him when they were young.

Or maybe it would be harder because when he saw her, he thought of his childhood.

It was uncomfortable for him to think of the past. Especially tonight, when it felt like they were building something new and different.

He wanted to share kisses with her and be absolutely certain she didn't see them as practice.

He just wasn't sure if it would work, and if she could feel the same.

Mike thought of the way she'd looked at him when she discovered the coffee shop in Nautilus. The way she hadn't been able to help herself from kissing him.

He nearly texted her to say he wanted to go on a real date.

But, no. He would be patient. See how the next few practice dates went, and hope she'd come to see him as the real thing. He also couldn't help hoping they'd do more practice kissing next time.

Not that Charlotte needed more practice. She'd already kissed him like that kraken had attacked the ship.

Totally obliterated him so that he'd forgotten himself and pulled her into his lap.

Yeah, he'd enjoy more of that.

Wednesday afternoon, Charlotte was working on a new dataset she'd received from a client. She'd imported the airborne EM data into her software and looked at it with maps of the area. Now, she selected a small section of data and tried developing a layered earth model. She started with a somewhat resistive half-space, then added additional layers in attempt to fit the decay curves.

But something wasn't right.

Did she have the wrong waveform settings and time channels?

Her phone rang. It was her parents.

"Hello," she said.

"Charlotte!" her father said. "What are you doing?"

"Um, you know I'm working."

This was the problem with working from home. People thought it meant she was always free. But Charlotte worked at least forty hours a week, and she kept fairly regular hours, so it was easy for her parents to avoid calling her then.

As she'd told them many times before.

There was no point telling them again. Besides, this data was frustrating her. She could use a break.

"We missed you this weekend," Dad said. "You should have come home for the long weekend."

"Both our girls in the city, and neither comes to visit us," Mom said. "It's not even a three-hour drive."

They must have her on speakerphone.

"I don't have a car, remember," Charlotte said. It was an unnecessary cost in Toronto, especially when she almost never left the apartment. "What's new in Ashton Corners?"

"The Jansens got a new puppy."

The Jansens were the couple who'd moved into Mike's house after his family left. They'd had two boys while Charlotte was in high school. Those boys would be in high school themselves now, wouldn't they?

It had been so many years since Charlotte had lived in Ashton Corners. Though she spent a lot of time alone, she preferred to be in a place that was bigger than a couple thousand people. Living in Toronto meant that when she did go out, she could frequent steampunk and cider bars, or eat udon and fancy ice cream.

She'd always thought of the Jansens' house as Mike's house. She'd resented them, even though they were perfectly nice—actually, that was part of the problem. They were a little too friendly, always trying to, God forbid, have conversations with her.

But worst part was that their presence meant Mike no longer lived next door. Where had his family moved to? She still hadn't asked him.

She opened her mouth to tell her mom that she'd run into Mike Guo, then wondered what on earth she was thinking. Mom would want a detailed description of everything he'd been up to for the last twenty years, and Charlotte still didn't know much about his life. There would be dozens of questions she'd answer with "I don't know," yet her mom would keep asking.

Nope, she wasn't going to tell her parents about meeting Mike, and she definitely wasn't going to say anything about the practice kissing.

Charlotte was thankful her parents still had their old landline, rather buying iPhones and FaceTiming her. She preferred it when they couldn't see her face.

"So, uh, how's the Jansens' new puppy?" she asked.

"Very cute, but such a troublemaker," Mom said. "Too hyper. Ruining our tomato plants. What's new in Toronto?"

"Oh, you know. Same old."

"I don't know why you live in Toronto when you never do anything exciting," Mom said. "Though the good thing about the city is that there are lots of available bachelors. How was your date the other week?"

"Mom, stop screeching in my ear."

"Fine, fine. You don't want to talk about it. I guess it wasn't very good, but do not give up hope." Mom paused. "I did have another question to ask you. I was cleaning out the basement. The set of Laurentien pencil crayons—do you want me to keep them?"

"Yes," Charlotte said immediately.

If her mother had asked her a month ago, she might have hesitated, but now those pencil crayons seemed important. Because they were part of her past with Mike.

God, when had she gotten so sentimental?

Mom clucked her tongue. "But you won't use them again. They will just collect dust in my basement for another twenty years."

"Next time I visit, I'll bring them back to Toronto with me, I promise. Put them in my old room."

"Have you seen Julie lately?" Dad asked.

"Tell her to call us," Mom said. "She seems to be avoiding our calls."

"Okay, I'll tell her," Charlotte said, though she hadn't seen her sister since the day of her first date with Mike, and they rarely texted.

"Maybe she's in trouble," Dad said. "We should go to Toronto for a visit."

"Please don't. I'm sure she's fine."

"You're right. Too much traffic. Better for you both to come here. What projects are you doing for work right now? We are telling everyone—"

"Not again," Charlotte muttered.

"—that you are very smart and have your own business in Toronto."

"A business of one person."

"You will get a boyfriend, and then we can brag about you even more!" Mom said.

Yes, Mom, I would like to get a boyfriend. However, I need some practice first...

Telling the truth was just asking for trouble.

Instead, Charlotte talked about her work a little, then got off the phone. She should return to her airborne data, but the mention of pencil crayons had reminded her of something.

A place she thought Mike would enjoy.

[10]

MIKE FOLLOWED Charlotte up the stairs to the second floor of the bar, remembering how, only five days ago, they'd gone upstairs at Nautilus and found that weird science lab.

Two days in a week with Charlotte. He felt lucky.

Today, she'd planned everything. For dinner, they'd gone out for hot pot, and now they were at this bar. He wasn't sure what was special about it, but Charlotte had insisted he'd like it.

She grabbed his hand and led him to two stools at the bar.

"What do you think?" she asked, holding up a container.

Mike couldn't respond. He was too distracted by the fact that he was sitting right next to her. He knocked his foot against hers, just because he could. He wanted to lean over and kiss her, but he'd save that for later.

She'd kissed him, though, on the walk here, and he'd told her that he was thrilled she was keeping up with her homework.

Finally, he focused on what was in her hand. It looked like a container that had once held frozen juice concentrate, now decorated with colored Popsicle sticks. Inside, there were crayons, and the bar was covered in butcher paper.

"Is this for drawing?" he asked stupidly.

"Yep. Over there"—she pointed at the far wall—"they display some of the cool things people have drawn over the years."

"They don't just draw colorful dicks?"

Charlotte flushed.

"Sorry," he said. "Didn't mean to make you uncomfortable. I was just noticing what the people at the other end of the bar were doing." He tilted his head to the right, at the group of guys who were drawing dicks in green and purple and laughing like they were so clever. They couldn't be older than twenty-five.

Mike and Charlotte each ordered a beer, and then he went to the wall of fame to look at what other customers had drawn. There was some truly spectacular art. A few portraits—hard to believe they'd been done with crayons. The Toronto skyline. An elephant.

Mike reminded himself that he didn't need to do anything spectacular. He was just supposed to have fun.

He returned to his seat and started drawing a kraken attacking a pirate ship. He and Charlotte drew together in silence for a few minutes, like they'd done so many times as children.

"Remember the day we met?" he said. "The day I moved in next door."

She nodded. "I was drawing with chalk on my driveway."

"You were drawing butterflies, if I remember correctly."

"Dear God, don't remind me that I used to be obsessed with butterflies."

"And I asked if I could draw with you. You said okay, and you pointed to the far end of the driveway and said that was my spot."

She laughed. "Yeah, I made you go as far away from me as possible."

But he hadn't cared. She was letting him draw with her, and that was enough for a boy who'd never been allowed to draw on the driveway before. "You complimented my tiger. I was very pleased."

"It was a fine tiger."

"Though you expressed skepticism that tigers could smile."

"Yeah, that part was a bit far-fetched."

That had been the beginning of their friendship, which had, especially at the beginning, included a lot of drawing. Always at her house. Charlotte had better art supplies, and at her place, nobody ever said their drawings were stupid. Her parents appreciated her interests and stuck her best drawings on the fridge. They seemed to like him, too, because he and Charlotte would draw quietly and play with Lego and never cause trouble.

To his parents, on the other hand, he was a constant disappointment. They complained that he was making them look bad, how could he do this to them? When they had come to this country for their children? He was always in trouble, often for tiny things, like making a mistake when he practiced piano. Or for things he hadn't even done, though they'd convince him that he had and force him to apologize.

He glanced at the Popsicle-stick crayon holder. He'd made something similar at school once and given it to his dad for Father's Day, because that was what his teacher had said they should do.

His teacher had praised his work, but his father had said it was ugly.

"Mike?" Charlotte said, pausing in her drawing. "Are you okay?"

"Yeah, I'm fine."

"If you don't want to draw, we don't have to. Or we can go somewhere else."

"No, no. I need to finish this kraken."

She placed her hand on his upper leg and squeezed, and her nearness wiped thoughts of his past out of his mind. She smelled like hot pot, and he was sure he did, too; the smell tended to linger.

He worked on his kraken for a while, though it was hard to

focus when she kept her hand on his leg. God, it really didn't take much, did it?

"I like your ship," she said, leaning over. "Too bad it's going to be demolished by the kraken and end up at the bottom of the ocean."

She planted a kiss on his cheek, and he turned toward her so he could kiss her on the lips, just once. Okay, maybe twice. He wasn't going for a full make-out session in front of the bartender, but it was hard to resist Charlotte.

He couldn't believe he got to kiss her.

And even though he was hardly an expert at such things and had mostly been talking out of his ass when he gave her "lessons," she still thought he was a good person to teach her about dating.

She'd always believed in him.

Charlotte, I want you for real.

It wasn't the right time to tell her. Not yet.

He was about to draw some eyes for the kraken—and maybe he'd make the kraken smile, just to give Charlotte a laugh—when he noticed what she was drawing.

"Is that an eggplant?" he asked, his voice laced with amusement.

A long eggplant, like ones he'd get from the Chinese grocer and use in stir-fries.

She looked down and stilled. As though she hadn't realized what she'd been drawing, her mind focused on something else while her hand moved of its own accord. She flushed again and covered her drawing with one hand.

Yep, she was thinking about it.

He glanced at the far end of the bar. The guys drawing dicks had left, but the dicks remained on the butcher paper. The largest of their dicks was purple, and there were balls with a few wiry red hairs at the base of it.

He turned back to Charlotte's drawing and moved her hand out of the way.

"Why are you thinking about eggplant?" he asked.

"Because I'm craving eggplant parmesan."

"We just had hot pot. And why are you drawing a whole eggplant, not eggplant parmesan?"

She shrugged. "Because it's difficult to draw eggplant parmesan."

"That never stopped you from trying to draw something before."

"I'm thirty-two now. Not six. I've changed."

"Yeah," he said softly, leaning in to whisper in her ear. "You have."

Charlotte's skin felt prickly and hot and uncomfortable.

Mike had made her aware of the fact she had needs. Needs that hadn't been fully satisfied in a long time. Sure, she did her best alone in her bedroom, but she was suddenly aware of how it would be astronomically better with him.

And now she found herself drawing stars on the butcher paper.

At least that was better than an eggplant. Why the fuck had she drawn an eggplant?

Well, she knew exactly why, and it had nothing to do with eggplant parmesan.

Even before Mike had whispered in her ear, she'd had... certain thoughts. While he'd been working on his kraken attacking a pirate ship—and occasionally looking at the bottles behind the bar with a glazed expression—she'd mostly been looking at him. Admiring. With every additional second, she found him even more attractive. Sometimes the longer you stared at something, the less sense it made.

But with Mike, things just became clearer.

Namely, the fact that he was really freaking handsome, and she had this weird urge to grab his arm muscles.

So, she hadn't been paying much attention to what she was drawing. Just doodling on the paper like she'd doodled during lectures in university.

Except in university, she'd mostly drawn geometric patterns.

"Are those balls?" Mike asked.

"They're apples, not balls," she protested.

"Of course," he murmured. "The eggplant has fruit for balls. Only sensible. But they look more like peaches to me." He smirked at her. "What were you thinking about?"

"Nothing! Absolutely nothing."

"Sure, I believe you."

"Stop doing that."

"What am I doing?" he asked.

"You know what you're doing. Pissing me off."

"I think it's amusing that you chose to draw an eggplant instead of, I don't know, a smiling tiger."

"I wasn't thinking about what I was drawing. It just happened."

"Ah. Your subconscious is trying to tell you something."

"I hate you." She crossed her arms over her chest like a petulant child.

"Nah, I think you like me very much and you're curious about my—"

"Don't say it!" she yelped.

"I know, I know. 'Eggplant' is such a dirty word. I shouldn't say it aloud."

"You're supposed to be giving me dating lessons."

"I am. We're flirting again."

She supposed they were. She bit her lower lip, just like he'd shown her on their first date.

His eyes, laser-focused on her lips, darkened.

Pleasure—and power—surged through her.

But then he snatched that power away by licking his lips. Slowly, obscenely. She imagined him doing that after he'd gone down on her.

She gasped.

God, he wasn't even touching her!

Then he placed his hand on her leg, above her knee. A simple touch that felt anything but simple; she was filled with an overwhelming need to get out of here.

"Let's go," she said, then chugged the last third of her beer.

"But I haven't finished my kraken."

"Fuck your kraken."

He shot her a look of mock outrage. "How dare you! At least let me add one more thing." He grabbed a purple crayon—which she'd used to draw that mortifying eggplant—and added a smile to his kraken.

She snorted before grabbing his hand and leading him down the stairs and out to the streets. It was a cool night for August, but her skin felt hot. Fortunately, she knew this area well, and there was a parkette nearby. She dragged him into the parkette and onto a bench that faced away from the street.

And then she kissed him. She wrapped her arms around him and pressed her mouth against his. He immediately dove into the kiss with enthusiasm and slid his hands into her hair.

Oh. That felt good, but it wasn't enough. She climbed onto his lap, not breaking the kiss.

"Still craving eggplant parmesan?" he asked. "Or are you craving something else?"

"Yes, I'm craving you, you dumbass."

She returned to kissing him, arching against his body as her hands slipped under the hem of his shirt. She'd touched him like this last weekend.

But today, he also slid his hands under her shirt, and she froze.

Noticing her reaction, he started to withdraw, but she clamped her hands on his wrists.

"I'm not used to this," she said. "It's been a while. But I want you to touch me. Yes."

"Here?" He toyed with the bottom of her bra.

"Yeah."

He eased his hand under one of her bra cups, brushing a callused finger over her nipple.

Had her nipples always been this sensitive, and she'd merely forgotten because it had been so long since someone else had touched them?

"Are my hands too rough?" he asked.

"No, no," she said quickly, not wanting him to stop. "Though why *are* they rough? It can't be related to your job."

"From the gym."

She took this as an invitation to feel his biceps, but then he brushed his finger over her nipple again, and she couldn't help squirming on his lap.

"I can feel your eggplant!" she exclaimed.

He turned away from her and barked out a laugh.

God, she was so bad at this. That was why she needed these lessons.

"Sorry," she said. "That wasn't sexy. I know. Rule seventy-three: Don't shout 'I can feel your eggplant!' while making out with a guy."

"What are the first seventy-two rules?"

"I don't know. Shut up and kiss me?"

Amusement danced in his eyes. They were doing that twinkling thing again.

He returned to kissing her and running his hands under her shirt. Her back, her stomach, and then her breasts. Somehow, his hands were just the right size, and when she shuddered in response to him squeezing her breast as he stroked her nipple, his body answered with a shudder of its own.

She needed to touch him *there*. He would be hot and hard for her and—

"...and then he projectile vomited and it was *awesome*."

"Dude, listen to you, using words like 'projectile.' That's some fancy-ass physics shit."

It was a bunch of guys walking past. Young guys, like the ones who'd drawn penises on the butcher paper.

She suddenly remembered they were on a park bench, a meter from the sidewalk of a major street.

She jumped up.

"You okay?" Mike asked.

"Yeah. Just remembered where we are."

"What do you want to do about that?"

Was he suggesting they go back to his place? Or hers? His place would be better because she didn't have condoms, though maybe he had some in his wallet...

"I, uh...I have to think about this," she said. "We should head home now. Separately. In case that wasn't clear."

"It's totally cool, Charlotte. Let's go to the subway."

He took her hand and guided her to the nearest subway station. Good thing he had his wits about him—she barely knew where they were.

His hand was on hers. His hand that had, just a minute ago, been on her breast.

She nearly made an embarrassing sound. She wanted him. She could go home with him.

No. She had to give herself time to think this through. That would be sensible.

Right?

[11]

CHARLOTTE ARRIVED at Ossington Cider Bar earlier than usual. None of her friends were here yet. Thanks to a bachelorette party, it was busy, and she had to wait for a table.

The women in the bachelorette party were all decked out in absurd outfits. The bride was easily identifiable because she was wearing a sash that said "bride" and had a tiara on her head.

A tiara? Charlotte would never wear one of those. *Just shoot me now.*

She wondered if they were going to a male strip club later. Or if they were from out of town and had gotten a suite in a hotel, and the maid of honor had arranged for a "cop" to knock on the door, responding to a noise complaint.

The cop, of course, would be a stripper, and he would dance to some ridiculous music. Perhaps he'd even do the Macarena.

Wait. Why was her mind conjuring up sexy images of Mike taking off a uniform?

She could totally see him doing it, though. Just for her. He'd have fun with it.

"Hey."

Charlotte nearly jumped.

"Sorry to startle you," said the white man standing beside her at the bar. There was a hint of uncertainty behind his smile, like he wasn't accustomed to talking to women in bars.

He was nice to look at. About her age. Curly chestnut hair. He wore khakis and a button-down shirt, and he had an iron ring on his pinky, so he must have studied engineering like her. Except she'd lost her ring several years ago and never replaced it.

"Can I buy you a drink?" he asked.

She almost laughed. A man was actually trying to pick her up! When was the last time this had happened?

It was exactly what she wanted, wasn't it? She wanted to get back into dating. She could talk to this guy for a few minutes, see what he was like.

But he must be at least six-four, and she was on the short side. It would be awkward to date someone who made her look tiny.

That was what she told herself as she shook her head and said, "Sorry, I have a boyfriend."

A moment later, the hostess guided her to a table, and Nicole showed up.

"Was that guy hitting on you?" Nicole asked, because of course Nicole had seen.

Sigh.

"Yes," Charlotte said.

"He's cute. Why did you tell him you had a boyfriend?"

"He's too tall."

"Are you listening to yourself?"

"Kissing would be awkward."

Unlike with Mike.

"So you're thinking about kissing," Nicole said. "Have you and Mike kissed?"

"Yeah—"

"I think you rejected this guy because you want Mike to be more than a practice date."

"No!" Charlotte scoffed.

"What's going on?" Sierra asked as she sat down. Rose and Amy had arrived, too.

"Someone tried to buy Charlotte a drink," Nicole said. "She declined because he was too tall. In other words, he's not Mike. And she and Mike have kissed."

"A practice kiss," Charlotte protested.

"How many practice kisses?"

"Um…" To be honest, she'd lost track.

"Has there been practice sex?" Nicole asked.

"No, but I think next weekend—"

"*You're going to have practice sex?*"

"It's only sensible. I haven't had sex in five years—"

"Which I admit I don't understand." Since her last relationship had ended nearly a decade ago, Nicole had slept with lots of different men and seemed to enjoy her lifestyle.

"Anyway, I could use a refresher," Charlotte finished.

"I think this has gotten a little out of control," Rose said. "It's clear you really like this guy, so why don't you tell him that?"

"Nope." Charlotte made a show of studying the tap list. There was a Golden Russet cider, which she'd had before. It was quite good. But she still read through the list of ciders that were too sweet for her.

In fact, she read it over five times.

"Charlotte…" Sierra said.

"Okay, fine. I like him a tiny bit as something other than a friend, and the kisses are very good, presumably just because I hadn't been kissed in a long time."

The words felt like a lie, but she'd stand by them.

"I see," Nicole said.

"It's too embarrassing to admit I caught feelings for a guy I'm practice dating," Charlotte said. "But they're only teeny-tiny feelings, just because we've been spending lots of time together and he's a nice guy, okay? I don't think it means anything."

"Then why did you turn down the other man just now? Other than his height."

"Gut instinct."

"Nothing wrong with gut instinct, but in this case, I think you're lying."

Charlotte rolled her eyes. "How do you never catch feelings for a guy you kiss? What's your secret?"

The server came around to take their orders. Fortunately, the server was not Julie.

When he walked away, Rose said, "I think having practice sex with a guy you have feelings for—"

"Teeny-tiny feelings," Charlotte clarified.

"—is dangerous. It might lead to even more feelings."

"Hmph."

What did Mike feel for her? He was fond of her in a friendly way, and he did seem somewhat attracted to her, but he'd been attracted to—and kissed—tons of women over the years, hadn't he? He was the sort of guy who got along with people easily, even grumpy hermits like her.

"Look, sex doesn't have to lead to feelings," Nicole said. "God knows I'd be in trouble otherwise. But if you're already feeling something for him, perhaps you should tell him."

"What if he's secretly in love with you, too?" Amy suggested. She was wearing a dress with freaking sunflowers on it. "Wouldn't that be the greatest?"

Charlotte considered the possibility for a split second before brushing it aside. "I highly doubt it."

"Tell us about your date yesterday," Sierra said. "What did you do?"

"We had hot pot then went to a bar where you can draw on the tables. They've got crayons and paper."

"Like Jack Astor's?"

"Yeah. Except not Jack Astor's. He drew a kraken attacking a ship. I drew..."

Ugh. She never should have started telling this story.

"You drew what?" Sierra asked, leaning forward.

"Yeah, based on your expression, this sounds good," Nicole said. "Let's hear it."

"An eggplant," Charlotte said morosely. "And some peaches that were…never mind."

"You drew an eggplant on your date?" Nicole snickered.

"I didn't know what I was doing!"

Thankfully, Charlotte's cider appeared in front of her at that moment. She immediately took a gulp.

And then a most unwelcome voice said, "You went on a date? With Mike again?"

Oh, no. Julie hadn't taken their order, but she was delivering their drinks.

"I'll confirm nothing," Charlotte said.

"Fine, fine, I won't bug you. For now." Julie handed out the rest of their drinks, and when she walked away to get another order, Charlotte finally let out her breath.

"Alright," Charlotte said. "Enough about my life for now."

"Just promise us you won't have practice sex with him," Sierra said.

"I promise."

This was a lie, but she didn't want her friends to keep bugging her.

Charlotte had become more keen on the idea and kept telling herself it was only sensible. Sex must be like other skills and required practice to be good at it, right? And she hadn't had sex since that nightmare of a proposal.

Yep. Very sensible to get a little practice. Have Mike give her some tips.

And her feelings for him were *very* tiny, weren't they? Sex wouldn't complicate matters.

Charlotte sipped her cider as she listened to Amy talk about her wedding, grimacing when the bride in the bachelorette party shrieked.

But then she thought about Mike sexily stripping and smiled.

"Whatcha thinking about Charlotte?" Sierra asked.

Oh, dear. Had she been smiling? How horrible.

"Nothing," Charlotte said. "Absolutely nothing."

But it's time to end my five-year dry streak.

MIKE'S PHONE BUZZED, and he pulled it out of his pocket, thinking it was Charlotte.

It wasn't Charlotte, but Angela, texting him a photo of one of Bailey's paintings. The poison dart frog, sitting on a leaf, was a striking shade of blue and had black spots. His niece certainly was talented.

Another image arrived a minute later. A painting of a spider.

Mike recoiled and dropped his phone.

"Something wrong?" Cody asked.

Mike and Mason were at Cody's apartment, hanging out and half watching a baseball game on TV. The Jays were playing the Angels, and there had yet to be any proposals.

Yes, that's good, Mike. Think about baseball rather than spiders from Australia.

Angela had helpfully included a brief description of the spider. Apparently, it was very dangerous.

Cody grabbed Mike's phone from the floor. "Damn. That's some spider."

"Please," Mike gasped. "Don't say the S-word!"

This, as intended, made his friends laugh.

Cody handed back the phone. "You okay? Even before you saw that drawing of a poisonous spider, you seemed a little off."

"It's venomous, not poisonous," Mike muttered. What the hell was wrong with him? The specifics didn't matter. It was one freaky-ass creature regardless. "Anyway, I'm fine."

Mason raised his eyebrows. "How's the woman you're seeing?"

Mike hesitated. "I'll tell you the truth. She thinks I'm an expert on dating—don't ask me how she arrived at that conclusion—and they're actually practice dates, not real ones. But the practice kissing—"

"Practice kissing?"

"Yep. It's getting rather heavy, and the thing is…I really like this woman. I told you that I knew her when we were kids, right? I had a big crush on her." He paused. "I don't think she feels the same way, even if she nearly came home with me."

"Did she, now?"

"A part of me is relieved it didn't happen, because she probably thinks I'm an expert at sex, too, and I didn't want to disappoint her."

"If she nearly came home with you," Cody said, "she must have found the practice kissing pretty good."

"She wanted me to give her kissing tips, though, and I just mumbled, 'don't go overboard on using your tongue.'"

Mason snickered. "Well, when you're doing certain things in bed, you definitely want to use lots of tongue, if you know what I mean."

Mike took out his imaginary notepad and pretended to write this down.

"I can't believe you're a dating coach." Cody laughed. "Look, if you have good chemistry, I'm sure it'll go fine. And you can be honest with her."

Mike wasn't sure how he felt about that. He rather liked Charlotte thinking he was a dating and sex god.

"But are you going to sleep with her," Mason said, "if she's interested in sex but doesn't have the same feelings for you?"

Mike scrubbed a hand over his face. "I'm not sure that would be a good idea...for me."

His friends didn't say he was ridiculous for how he felt.

Instead, Cody slapped him on the back and said, "I hope it goes well for you, bro." He helped himself to some pretzels and beer and let out a burp that would have been really cool if they were, like, eight.

Although Mike's gaze was now on the TV, he kept thinking about Charlotte.

For their fifth practice date, Mike took Charlotte to his favorite sushi restaurant, and he learned something new about her: she really, really liked spicy salmon rolls.

He added this to his mental folder of things he knew about Charlotte Tam.

Afterward, he took her to Harbord Coffee Bar.

"Their roll cakes are good," Charlotte said as he opened the door for her.

He couldn't help feeling a little disappointed. He'd wanted to take her somewhere she'd never been. In a city as large as Toronto, that shouldn't be too hard, should it?

"Is something wrong?" she asked as they waited in line.

"You've been here before."

She squeezed his hand. "You're taking me out for coffee and dessert. How could I be sad about that?"

It didn't feel like they were on a *practice* date, but...

She ordered a latte with a double shot of espresso, and he ordered a decaf latte.

They sat on the bench seating with their drinks, a single slice of dark chocolate raspberry roll cake, and two forks. He rested his arm behind her, and she looked up at him and smiled.

God, she could practically make the air *whoosh* out of him with just a smile.

She was wearing a black shirt, and her hair was pulled back with a clip behind one ear. He liked the asymmetrical look.

She stabbed the cake with her fork, but rather than bringing the bite of cake to her own mouth, she held it to his lips.

"This is an appropriate thing to do on a date, isn't it?" she said. "Feeding each other?"

"Uh, yeah." It was hard to form words when she was so close to him.

He wrapped his lips around the fork. It was chocolate sponge cake with a creamy chocolate filling and fresh raspberries, and it tasted like the best thing ever.

"When I was a kid," he said, "I vowed that when I grew up, I would eat a lot of cake."

She chuckled. "And have you?"

"Not nearly enough," he said soberly.

Yes, eating cake with Charlotte. This was basically his dream.

If only he could do it every day.

"When did you start drinking coffee?" he asked.

The next bite of cake went into her own mouth, and she made a hum of approval that vibrated inside him.

"In high school," she said. "By the way, where did you go to high school? Where did you move after Ashton Corners?"

"Etobicoke."

"So, you've been in the city for a long time."

Yes, he had. But he didn't want to think about his past today. Not that part of it, anyway.

He pressed a quick kiss to Charlotte's lips.

"You taste like chocolate," she murmured.

"I hope you're not complaining."

"How could I possibly complain about that?" She sipped her latte. "Mmm. Chocolate and coffee go so well together."

"Yes, it's a great combination."

"But your latte is decaf." She wrinkled her nose.

"It tastes perfectly fine, I assure you. The barista even made a little heart on top. Isn't it cute?"

She tried his latte and wrinkled her nose again. "Nope."

"Can you really tell the difference?" he asked.

"Of course. I'm an expert when it comes to caffeine."

"Mm-hmm."

"Why do you sound skeptical? You've seen me drink a damn lot of coffee."

"I suppose I have."

It was hard to focus when the column of her neck was right there, begging to be kissed.

And kiss it he did. A fairly chaste kiss, as far as kisses to the neck went.

"I'm disappointed in you for your decaf latte," she said.

"I don't want to be up all night."

"Well, I was sort of hoping…you would."

The air in the coffee shop suddenly seemed heavy. Did she mean what he thought she meant?

"You want me to be up all night," he said slowly.

"Was that a terrible line?" She worried her bottom lip.

"No, I like it." He nodded. "I like it."

"So, it's working on you?" She put a hand on his leg and slid it up, just a little. "Excellent. When I proposed this practice-dating business, I didn't really imagine practice sex, however…"

It was like he'd been doused in cold water.

He looked down at the half-eaten cake and had a bite. It wasn't as good as it had been a few minutes ago.

"What's wrong?" she asked. "I thought you'd be into it, but if not, I understand, don't worry. I've had a week to think about it, and—"

"And you've been envisioning what sex with me would be like?"

"Yeah. But also thinking about it practically. It'll be fun for both of us, right? Plus, it'll give me some good experience."

God, this was painful.

He took a deep breath. Time to make his feelings clear.

"Charlotte," he said, "I won't have *practice* sex with you."

"Okay, that's—"

"If we're going to sleep together, it has to be real."

[13]

"Practice sex is still real sex," Charlotte stammered.

This conversation was not going the way she'd expected.

Mike was looking at her in an odd way, in a way he'd never looked at her before. There was no trace of humor or lightheartedness in his expression. He looked *fierce*.

She felt a strange thrill down her spine.

"What I'm trying to tell you," he said, "is that I can't have meaningless sex, not with you. If we have sex, it's going to *mean* something to me."

"Oh."

"*Oh*, indeed. You're going on about practice dates and practice kisses and practice sex, but I can't go along with that anymore. I had a crush on you when we were younger, and since meeting up with you again… Well, I want you. In my bed, yes, but more than anything, I want you to see me as something more than your practice date."

She sat there, stunned.

She had not expected this.

"You're serious?" she whispered, even though she knew he was, but she was still wrapping her mind around this.

"Of course I'm serious. The way you draw eggplants with peaches for balls, the way you insult my taste in cider and lattes—it drives me fucking mad. The way you kiss me..." He shook his head.

She didn't say anything.

He stuffed a big bite of cake in his mouth, drained his caffeine-free latte, and stood up.

The loss of him next to her—she felt it acutely.

He felt this way about her? Mike, the boy who'd draw and play by her rules?

"You had no idea back then, did you?" he said.

She shook her head. Julie had said he'd had a crush on Charlotte, but Charlotte hadn't believed it.

"And now..." he began.

"Now I..."

"It's fine. I never expected you to feel the same way."

But it wasn't fine. She could see it in the taut lines in his face, and she hated to see Mike looking like this.

And that wasn't all.

Because she *had* been thinking that she had teeny-tiny feelings for him.

She clutched his wrist before he could leave. "You took me to a baseball game, and despite my bad experience the previous time, I had fun. You understood me. You took me to a cool bar and..."

God, she was just listing dates they'd gone on. Dates he'd planned specifically for her, and that wasn't so remarkable, but after all those stories of shitty first dates, it had seemed rather remarkable.

It was more than that, though.

She couldn't explain it.

"If you could let me go," he said tensely, "I'd appreciate it."

"But I do...I do have feelings for you." It was hard to choke out the words, but he needed to know the truth. "I didn't mean to fall for the guy who was teaching me how to date, but it happened all the same. I told myself it was no big deal, just teeny-tiny feelings, but that's a lie. They're not tiny."

When she thought of him walking out of her life again… Yes, she knew she felt more than she'd assumed earlier.

"You…" He sat down again, looking a little dazed. "You really want this? No more practicing?"

"Yeah." She twisted her hands in her lap. "I can't make any long-term promises, and I haven't been in a relationship for a while, so maybe I'm terrible at it, but I want to try. If that's enough for you."

"It's enough."

In the subsequent silence, they both breathed heavily.

"You want to get out of here?" she asked.

He responded by grabbing her hand, and she followed him out of the coffee shop, not even bothering to finish her latte.

And *that* was truly shocking.

They went to his apartment because it was closer.

When they stumbled into his bedroom, Charlotte slipped her hands under Mike's shirt and pulled it over his head. She ran her hands over his chest and growled in frustration.

"What is it?" he asked.

"I want to see you."

He flicked on the lights, and she had her fill of him. He wasn't bulky, but he was muscled in lots of great places.

And then she couldn't see him anymore because he was pulling her shirt over her head, followed by her bra.

Afterward, he looked like he'd been stunned into speechlessness.

He likes me.

It was such a heady feeling, to have that returned. Like she was high, except the one time she'd gotten high, it hadn't been much fun. She'd—

She gasped as he dipped his head and sucked her nipple into his mouth. A jolt went right to her core. Surely she'd felt something like this before, but it had been so long since she'd been touched this way, and never had it been with Mike.

He shifted his attention to her other breast before lifting his head, a wicked smile on his face that nearly melted her into a puddle. He placed both of his hands on her cheeks and kissed her mouth; it was exquisitely needy and intimate. Then he walked her backward until her calves hit the side of the bed, and she toppled onto it.

He followed her, and he just kept kissing her and kissing her.

"I want this to be so good for you," he murmured.

"I have no doubt it will be."

"Just stop me if you ever need to, okay? Don't be shy. You can boss me around. That's fine, too."

At his invitation, she grabbed his hand and placed it on the button of her jeans. He opened them up and slipped his hand into her underwear.

"Charlotte. God."

He slid his fingers through her wetness as he kissed her, and she arched against him. She considered making a comment about his eggplant, but in the end, she simply unzipped his jeans and reached into his boxers.

She closed her eyes and felt how hard he was.

Yes, this was definitely a heady feeling.

He wiggled her jeans and underwear down her hips and tossed them aside. She hadn't been naked with a man in so long, but she wasn't uncomfortable. Not with him.

He circled her entrance with a fingertip. It was excruciating; she needed more.

And then two long fingers thrust inside her, and she let go of him, practically mindless. She squirmed and murmured incoherent words as he took a nipple between his lips again.

Oh, God. She couldn't keep track of everything he was making her feel. She just knew it was *good*.

When he slid downward, she tensed in anticipation.

Still, when he swirled his tongue over her clit, she was shocked by the sharpness of the sensation.

He licked her lazily, as though taking all the time in the world to savor her.

She fisted the blankets. "Mike…"

He looked up at her, which was a shame because he wasn't licking her anymore. But the way his eyes were blazing, the intensity of his gaze…

She swallowed. "You like it when I say your name."

"Yeah, Charlotte, I do."

Then he licked her with abandon, and she gripped the blankets even more tightly and thrust up to meet him. When she came, she shattered as she never had before.

He raised himself up and crawled toward her, licking his lips. Last weekend, she'd imagined him doing just that after going down on her.

Frantically, she shoved off his pants and boxers. She took his cock in her hand and watched his face as she pumped once. Twice.

"Like I told you," she said, "I'm terribly out of practice, so…"

He hissed out a breath. "Don't worry, you're doing fucking great. Too great, actually. If I blow my load before I'm inside you…"

He fumbled for something in his night table. She watched as he tore open the packet and rolled the condom onto his cock.

"Do you want more lube?" he asked.

She nodded. Probably a good idea, even as wet as she was. It had been a damn long time, and he was…well, not a fucking giant, but a pretty good size.

He pulled out a squeeze tube of lube, and she took it from his hands and tried to squeeze some onto her fingers. But nothing came out, even though it was nowhere close to empty.

He unscrewed the lid and pulled off the foil covering.

Oh. It was new. When was the last time he'd…

She was distracted by him applying the lube. He wiped his hands on a tissue and positioned his cock at her entrance. She felt unsteady and *desperate*.

He slid inside, just a little. "Okay?"

She nodded. She grabbed his ass—ooh, that was nice—and pulled him farther inside. He shut his eyes, as if overcome, and she felt a deep rush of affection…and desire. When she wrapped her legs around his waist, he pushed the rest of the way inside.

It was too much, too much.

At the same time, it was just perfect.

He started to move inside her, and she clutched him against her, needing all of him. She pushed her hand through his hair and brought his head down to hers, kissing him as he moved. Such a glorious feeling.

She'd forgotten just how wonderful sex could be.

He bit her lip lightly, and that caused another jolt of pleasure. His mouth moved to her breast again, and God, that was amazing, too.

He rocked faster. "I think I'm…"

His body shook against hers, and she touched every inch of skin that she could.

"Charlotte," he said quietly, and her name reverberated through her, even as he rolled onto his side. "Next time, I'll last longer. I promise."

"When's next time?"

"Whenever you want it to be."

"You should have had a big latte so we could do this all night. None of that decaf shit."

"Don't you worry. I don't need caffeine, not when I have you here."

After they cleaned up, she returned to bed with him, and he put his arm around her and pulled her against his side.

Somehow, she'd completely forgotten about this part of a relationship. There was kissing. There was sex. But there were other kinds of touching, too. Like post-coital cuddling.

It was surprisingly comfortable, given she was so used to being alone.

He propped himself up on his elbow. "So, was it...okay for you?"

He sounded uncertain.

She thought of the unopened lube. "When was the last time you had sex?"

"It was a while ago, yeah." This was accompanied by an uncharacteristically nervous laugh. "Not five years, but I'm sure you've had much more sex than I have, since you were in a long-term relationship. I've never had anything that lasted close to a year."

"Nor were you picking up lots of women in bars and having one-night stands?"

"Nah, not so much."

"But you..." Then she realized that he'd never said he had lots of experience with dating. She'd just assumed.

"You were so keen on the idea of me teaching you," he said, "and I thought maybe it would be good for me, too. Give me practice at dating, getting close to someone. I'm sorry I misled you. I should have told you earlier. If you're pissed, I understand."

She felt a moment of annoyance that he hadn't told her, but that wasn't what troubled her the most.

"It's fine," she said. "Don't worry about it. But you're cute and charming and easygoing. I thought surely people would be lining up to be with you."

Or perhaps he'd been pushing them away.

Huh.

But they were here together now, in bed, and he'd asked a question she had yet to answer.

"It was really great for me," she said, "and I'm not just saying that for your ego."

"Yeah, that wouldn't be like you." He paused. "I was hoping to make you come more than once."

"I'm always happy with once. And I never come just from penetration. You'd have to...you know."

"Ah. I should have been thinking about these things. I just..." He gestured vaguely.

"I was so hot that I made your brain stop functioning. Yeah, yeah, I get it." It was weird for her to talk about how hot she was, but it was clear he saw her that way.

He laughed. "Something like that."

It was nice to hear him laugh again.

"Any tips for me?" she asked. "After all, you were supposed to be the one teaching *me*."

"I don't want to hear about practice kissing and practice sex ever again," he growled, rolling her underneath him.

As soon as he did that, she realized she'd said those words partly to get under his skin. Like when she teased him about decaf coffee. But teasing him when they were both naked and he could easily roll on top of her...or kiss her...or suck on her nipple...

Yeah, it was kind of thrilling. And the thought that he liked her made Charlotte a touch giddy, and fuck, she was not the kind of person who did things like *giddiness*.

She wanted to clarify a few things first, though.

"No more practice dates," she said, "but where do we go from here?"

"I'm not sure. You now know I'm hardly an expert at such things. Take it slow and see where it goes, I guess?"

"Sounds good to me."

"I promise I won't date anyone else. There's no one but you."

He bent down and kissed her on the lips.

"What should we do now?" she asked. "You got any ideas?"

"I have tons of ideas."

And, indeed, he did.

[14]

CHARLOTTE WOKE up to an ear-piercing shriek.

What the hell? Was there a burglary?

She bolted upright, and the blanket fell down. She instinctively covered her breasts with her arms, not wanting the burglar to see her naked.

Except the blankets were unfamiliar. Where was the quilt that her mother had made? Had the burglar stolen it?

No, the shrieking was coming from Mike. She was at Mike's apartment.

"What's wrong?" she asked him.

He was clutching the blankets and looking at the wall. He seemed incapable of proper speech and merely pointed.

It looked like a bug of some sort. She stood up and walked over to it.

"It's just a spider," she said.

"Yes, it's a fucking spider."

"You're still scared of spiders?"

"What does it look like?"

"I'll get rid of it, don't worry." Charlotte grabbed a tissue from his dresser. "Come here, little spider, I won't hurt you."

Once she had the spider in hand, she walked to the washroom, but not to flush the spider down the toilet. Instead, she grabbed a towel to cover herself, then brought the spider to Mike's balcony and flicked it from the tissue onto the railing.

"Go on," she said. "Find somewhere else to live and catch all sorts of delicious insects."

When she returned to the bedroom, Mike covered his face with his hands.

"Don't worry, it's gone," she said.

"This isn't how I expected the morning to go."

"What did you imagine?"

"I don't know. Something more romantic than me waking you up with a scream? This is the first time I've seen a spider in this apartment."

"Spiders are useful." She dropped the towel and slid into bed beside him. "They eat other things you might not want. And their webs are pretty cool."

"Yeah, you've told me before. It doesn't change anything. Plus, spiders can be poisonous. Sorry, venomous."

"Not sure we have any venomous spiders in Canada, unless they're escaped pets."

"Thanks for that."

"I'm happy to remove all your spiders." She patted his shoulder. "I'm obligated to like spiders, since I was named for one."

This earned her a chuckle. "Right. I forgot about that."

Charlotte had been born less than a year after her parents had arrived in Canada. As the story went, they were at her aunt and uncle's house when her mom was five or six months pregnant. Her aunt and uncle had been in Canada for several years and had a little girl, who was eight at the time: Charlotte's cousin Sara. When they were discussing baby names, Sara said she was reading a famous book with a character named Charlotte, and wasn't that a nice name?

Charlotte's mother thought that yes, it was pretty, and when

Sara mentioned that the character was very clever, the baby's fate had been sealed.

If they had a girl, she'd be named Charlotte.

Of course, Sara had failed to mention that this very clever character in this very famous book was actually a spider…until Charlotte's first birthday.

Okay, so Charlotte hadn't precisely been named for a spider, but she'd gotten her name because of *Charlotte's Web*.

"Does it bother you to be dating a woman with a spider's name?" she asked.

"I think I'll manage." Mike smiled at her. "God, I'm embarrassed. Honestly, spiders are the only thing I'm afraid of."

"How convenient that I was here to act as your spider-removal service."

"It certainly was." He kissed her cheek. "Did you sleep well?"

She hesitated. "I'm not used to sharing a bed. It took me a while to fall asleep."

"I'm sorry. I could have slept on the couch—"

"No, no. It's fine." She'd gotten to lie in bed next to him, still feeling the tiniest bit giddy. She supposed she'd get used to this soon enough.

"How about I make you breakfast?" he said. "What do you usually have?"

"Usually I stumble out of bed and make coffee, then dump some cereal into a bowl."

"Pancakes? Scrambled eggs and bacon? Whatever you like."

She nearly told him not to bother, even though both sounded delicious. Someone else cooking breakfast for her seemed like too big of an imposition.

But he had an eager look on his face, and if he wanted to cook for her, she'd let him.

Damn, he was cute. And the fact that he wasn't wearing a shirt was certainly helping.

"Pancakes," she said.

~

Charlotte sang in the shower.

Mike added this to his list of things he knew about her.

Loves spicy salmon rolls. Looks really good naked. Not afraid of spiders. Sings Disney songs in the shower.

Yes, she was singing "Beauty and the Beast."

Then she immediately launched into "Gaston."

Even though she had a lovely voice, she'd probably be mortified if she knew he could hear her from the kitchen.

He didn't make pancakes often. It felt lavish to make them just for himself, but Charlotte was in his apartment. He was glad she'd chosen pancakes, but he would have happily made whatever she liked.

God, he still couldn't believe this was happening.

It had taken a lot of courage to tell her that he didn't want to be her practice sex partner, and he'd expected rejection, even as he poured out his feelings.

And now, here he was. Making pancakes and coffee for her.

Several minutes later, Charlotte appeared, wearing nothing but a towel.

He nearly pinched himself to make sure this wasn't a dream.

When she took a seat at the breakfast bar, he placed a large cup of coffee in front of her, and she looked at him with gratitude.

He tried not to think about the fact that he'd shrieked over a spider. At the very least, he should have uttered a long string of curse words instead.

"I like your outfit," he said. "A short, strapless dress made of fluffy blue fabric. Very fashionable."

"Your towels are indeed very fluffy."

"Thank you for complimenting my *towels*."

When he waggled his eyebrows, she laughed.

Seriously, how was this real?

He flipped her pancakes onto a plate and placed it in front of her, along with appropriate cutlery. Next, he grabbed the butter and bottle of maple syrup.

"Real maple syrup," she said.

"Of course. You should always have the best."

"Brad preferred butter-flavored table syrup. Store brand."

"He *preferred* that? And he's Canadian?"

Charlotte laughed again, and Mike started on the next batch of pancakes, feeling uneasy.

She'd mentioned her ex, who'd been with her for three years.

Mike shouldn't be bothered. It was a casual comment, and after Brad, Charlotte had sworn off dating for five years. The idiot had publicly proposed to her at a fucking baseball game. He was no competition for Mike, who was making her pancakes with real maple syrup for breakfast.

Had Brad made her pancakes? With his stupid table syrup? How many times had they eaten breakfast together like this?

Charlotte was entitled to have a past, and Brad was firmly in the past. But Mike couldn't help thinking about how he didn't have a past like she did.

While she'd dated, he'd been in therapy, trying to straighten out his messed-up thoughts.

He poured himself a cup of coffee and turned back to Charlotte as his pancakes cooked.

"You might enjoy this." He flipped to Angela's latest messages on his phone. "My niece did them. I can't say I spent more than a second looking at the spider, though."

Charlotte took the phone. "They're very good." She paused. "Does your sister have any other kids? Is she married?"

"Not anymore."

Angela had gotten married while in university. She'd been eager to escape their parents. But her marriage hadn't been healthy, and she'd been divorced for many years now.

"How are your mom and dad?"

He clenched the spatula. "Alive, as far as I know. I don't talk to them anymore."

"Shit, I'm sorry for bringing it up."

Since they were in a relationship of sorts now, was he obligated to provide details?

Not yet, he figured. And it wasn't like she knew nothing. He hadn't talked much about his home life as a kid, but they'd always hung out at her place, and she'd had some idea.

"I'm out of practice at this morning-after business," she said.

"Me, too. Don't worry about it."

They smiled at each other.

A few minutes later, he had his pancakes on a plate, loaded with lots of maple syrup—today was a special occasion, after all —and they were eating together.

"Do you have any plans for today?" he asked.

Charlotte pulled something out of her purse. A little day planner, from the looks of it. The illustration on the front was of a large tree with gears in its trunk and among its twisted roots. It reminded him of Nautilus.

She flipped to this week's pages, and to his surprise, they were covered in cute stickers.

She immediately closed the day planner.

"Nope, nothing planned for today," she said in a rush.

He gently pulled the planner from her hands and opened it to the first page. There was a border of delicate blossom stickers.

"These are nice," he said.

She glowered at him.

"What?" he said. "I like them."

"Don't be sarcastic."

"I'm not being sarcastic. They're nice stickers. Not what I was expecting, but—"

"Exactly." She pulled the planner away from him and stuffed it in her plain black purse. "They are most un-Charlotte-like."

"I was right. You do talk about yourself in the third person."

She gulped her coffee. "There isn't enough caffeine in my bloodstream to talk about my cutesy planner."

"Nothing to be embarrassed about. But I'm happy to serve you more caffeine." He picked up the coffeepot and poured the rest of the coffee in her mug. "You know what we can talk about instead? Rather than my family and your wicked awesome planner?"

"What?"

"The precarious knot holding up your towel dress." He touched a finger to the knot just above her breasts.

"Yeah, you're interested in that, aren't you?"

"Very interested in what I could do once I undid it with a flick of my fingers."

Once they finished their pancakes and coffee, they spent the rest of the morning in bed.

[15]

CHARLOTTE WAS ABOUT to spend some quality time with Netflix when her phone buzzed. She picked it up immediately, smiling at the thought of a text from Mike. She'd just seen him a few hours ago, and she was already eager to hear from him again.

But the text wasn't from him, and she tried not to be disappointed.

Did you have practice sex with Mike last night? Nicole asked.

Charlotte typed a quick response. *Nah, he told me he liked me and we had sex of the non-practice variety.*

To her surprise, she didn't get a response.

Probably for the best.

Now wearing her favorite pair of pajama shorts, a geology shirt, and no bra, she made some coffee and fired up a particularly gruesome, twisted movie to make up for all her sappy feelings.

Charlotte was halfway through the movie when someone knocked on the door. People rarely knocked on her door without notice, with the exception of political canvassers during election season. No reason to answer.

"I know you're in there," said a familiar voice. "I can hear you watching a movie."

"Nobody's home," Charlotte muttered.

Which was, of course, the worst way to convince someone that nobody was home.

Sighing, she paused the movie and opened the door.

To her horror, Nicole, Rose, and Amy immediately walked in and took off their shoes. Three people in her quiet apartment.

Argh.

Sierra had probably wanted to come, too, but she'd be at work.

"What's this about?" Charlotte asked, even though she knew the answer.

"We want to hear about your night," Rose said.

"I sent a text to Nicole."

"A very intriguing text," Nicole said. "Only one sentence, and we want details."

"Of course you do." Charlotte went to the kitchen and poured some Baileys into her second cup of coffee. She also brought out a bag of salt and vinegar chips.

"A kind gentleman held the door for us," Amy said, "so that's why you didn't have to buzz us in." She gestured to the TV. "What are you watching?"

"Just something light about serial killers to calm myself down."

The frozen image on-screen was particularly gory. Charlotte turned off the TV so as not to further offend her friends' delicate sensibilities. She sat down on the couch. Rose and Nicole joined her, and Amy grabbed a chair from the dining room table.

"So, how was the sex?" Nicole asked. "Was it enjoyable non-practice sex?"

"It was acceptable," Charlotte said.

Unfortunately, after her terse answer, she couldn't help smiling.

Goddammit.

Stupid Mike, giving her stupid orgasms and making her feel good.

"Looks like it was amazing." Nicole nudged Charlotte's shoulder.

"I want to hear about how he confessed his feelings," Rose said.

"Well, I suggested we have practice sex—"

"You did not."

"I did. And he said no, he couldn't have sex with me without it meaning something. And apparently he had a crush on me when we were younger."

"How sweet! He's been pining after you all these years."

"I highly doubt it," Charlotte said. "Though he's not as experienced with dating and sex as I'd assumed."

"As I said, he's been pining after you for years."

"Can I get back to my movie now?"

"Very funny," Nicole said. "You have guests to entertain."

"So, your feelings for him aren't purely *plu*tonic?" Amy said.

Charlotte frowned.

"Your shirt." Amy gestured toward it.

Charlotte looked down at the shirt she never wore out of the apartment. It said "My Feelings are Purely Plutonic" and had an illustration of a rock.

"What are plutonic rocks again?" Nicole asked. "We must have learned about them in that geology course we all had to take in first year, but I remember almost nothing from it, except the prof always brought a hockey stick to class."

"They're a type of igneous rock," Rose said, "aren't they?"

"Igneous rocks that form below the surface," Charlotte said. "As opposed to extrusive rocks, which form at the surface. Crystal size—"

"We did not come here for a geology lecture," Nicole said.

That was unfortunate. Charlotte would prefer geology over their previous topic of conversation.

"Are those salt and vinegar chips?" Amy asked, making a face.

"Yeah," Nicole said. "Charlotte's favorite."

"Gross."

"Look," Charlotte said. "I didn't invite you over to insult my chips and interrupt my geology lectures. In fact, I didn't invite you over at all."

"I know, I know," Nicole said. "Which is why we aren't staying long. But it's not every day a guy declares his love for you—"

"He didn't declare his love for me."

"Okay, declared his like. Whatever. Anyway, it's exciting news."

Charlotte would never admit it—God, no—but it actually was somewhat exciting that her friends were here. Though she certainly wasn't going to spill lots of details about Mike, it was nice to talk about him…a little.

"Are you in a relationship?" Amy asked.

"Yes."

Amy bounced in her seat. "This is such great news!"

"Indeed." Charlotte grabbed her poor rejected salt and vinegar chips, stuffing some into her mouth.

"I'll put him down as your plus one for my wedding. It's less than a month away, and I need to confirm the numbers soon."

To her annoyance, Charlotte liked the idea of Mike being her date for a wedding. And Amy's wedding wasn't all that far off. They'd still be seeing each other then, right?

"Let me ask him first," she said.

"Excellent." Amy beamed.

"We've seen him before, but we haven't really met him," Nicole said. "We need to ask him lots of questions. Make sure he's good enough for you."

Charlotte instantly felt protective of Mike. "Uh, go easy on him."

"Well, clearly we didn't do a good enough job with the last one. He proposed to you at a ballgame and he preferred table syrup to maple syrup."

"I can't believe you remember that."

"I can't help it. It was so shocking."

"Don't worry, Mike gave me real maple syrup with my pancakes this morning."

"I like this guy already," Rose said.

Okay, it was nice that her friends were looking out for her, but Charlotte had reached her socializing quota for the day.

As if understanding this, Rose stood up. "We'll get out of your hair so you can watch something with blood and murder."

"The description even promised cannibalism," Charlotte supplied helpfully.

"Or you could join us for a late lunch," Amy said. "There's a restaurant nearby with Ojibway-style tacos."

"No, that's okay. I'll stay here with my movie and salt and vinegar chips. What kind of chips do you like?"

"Sour cream and onion," Amy answered.

"Those are my second favorite."

"And dill pickle."

"Dear God, get her out of here."

A few minutes later, everyone was out the door and Charlotte was back to enjoying her movie and the dregs of her coffee.

And, okay, thinking about Mike in peace.

After dinner, Charlotte tidied up her bedroom. Not that her bedroom was a pigsty, but she'd probably have company here soon, and it could do with a little cleaning. She was putting away the duster when her phone buzzed. She reached for it a little less eagerly than last time.

But this time, it was Mike.

Thinking of you, he said.

Aw, wasn't that sweet.

In fact, he texted a moment later, *I'm doodling eggplants on my notepad.*

He followed this up with an eggplant emoji, then a photo of his doodled eggplants.

Those are very fine eggplants, she said.

She debated whether to add a winky face, ultimately deciding against it. But she went to her desk and drew an eggplant on her little notepad, just because.

And then she found herself doodling hearts.

WTF. What was happening to her?

She felt slightly off-kilter and out of control. She couldn't remember ever feeling like this before, although perhaps she'd just forgotten, seeing as the last time she'd started a relationship was eight years ago.

It was unsettling.

Charlotte liked her usual routine. Change was scary.

But you want this, she reminded herself, *and he's good to you, even if he woke you up by screaming because he'd seen a spider.*

She took a deep breath, then sent him a text about Amy's wedding.

They were supposed to take things slow, but even though it had only been a day, Mike had already texted Charlotte to say he was thinking of her, and he'd agreed to be her date for a wedding. He wouldn't deny that he'd grinned like an idiot when she'd invited him.

What was the etiquette for the early stages of a relationship? Should he text her every day? Would that be too much? How many eggplant doodles should he send her before it started to seem really weird?

He was out of his depth.

You're going to screw this up, Mike. You think you're good enough for her? Ha!

He pushed that aside and reminded himself of all the things he'd done that his parents had said he'd never be able to do.

When his phone buzzed, he leapt to check it.

When will I get to see your eggplant again? Charlotte asked.

He wanted to tell her to come over right now but settled for suggesting next weekend.

Then he called Mason to ask for more restaurant advice and tell him that he and Charlotte had progressed from practice dates to real dates.

It was good to have people in his life who were actually happy for him and didn't think he'd screw everything up. He'd come a long way from his childhood in Ashton Corners.

But the best part of his childhood, Charlotte Tam, was part of his life again. He'd try his hardest to do right by her, and hopefully not scream the next time he saw a spider in her company.

[16]

"Would you like to hear today's specials?" the server asked.

"Sure." Mike smiled at him.

"For our appetizer, we have a burrata caprese salad, and for our pizza of the day, we have our posh Hawaiian pizza."

"Ooh, tell me more about the pizza."

Across the table, Charlotte glared at him rather comically.

The server seemed to have similar feelings about Hawaiian pizza. He let out a small, world-weary sigh. "It has grilled pineapple, prosciutto, fresh mozzarella, and arugula."

"I'll have that one, please," Mike said.

"And for you?" The server turned to Charlotte.

She pointed to the pizza she wanted on the menu. It had porcini and sausage.

It did not sound as good as the special.

When the server left, Charlotte said, "I can't believe you ordered Hawaiian pizza."

"It's not Hawaiian pizza," Mike said. "It's *posh* Hawaiian pizza."

"Mm-hmm. What is it with you and fruit on pizza?"

He shrugged and had a sip of his cider. "I can't believe you ordered Get Out of My Trash! again."

She pressed a hand to her chest and looked outraged. "It's a very sophisticated cider."

"Sure it is."

"Well, I've had this cider fewer times than you've had Hawaiian pizza."

"That's just due to lack of opportunity. Besides, I'm having *posh* Hawaiian pizza, remember."

"It doesn't sound like you'll let me forget, does it?" she muttered.

Then she met his eyes over her glass and smiled.

He laced his fingers with hers. "I'm glad we're doing this again."

"Me, too. Even if we're not doing it properly, due to your unfortunate taste in pizza. The server didn't seem impressed."

Perhaps she'd shut up about this if he kissed her.

However, they were seated on opposite sides of the table, and he'd have to save that for later. He settled for sliding his other hand up her leg, just above the inside of her knee. Her lips parted slightly.

The best part? He knew it was all real.

Mike had debated between many restaurants for their first real date. Mason had told him of a tapas place that sounded good, as well as an upscale barbecue restaurant. But in the end, he'd decided they should go back to the site of their first practice date and redo it as a real date.

So here they were, at Anne's in the Junction. By coincidence, they were even seated at the same table.

Insulting each other's food and beverage choices was somehow different, now that he'd kissed her, now that this was real for both of them.

Charlotte looked particularly lovely tonight. Rather preppy, with a short-sleeved white shirt, an argyle vest, and a headband.

Yes, he was very much digging her look.

"I'm surprised you didn't get the roasted eggplant pizza," he said.

"What are you—*oh*." She snorted. "We're so mature."

"We are."

He held up his glass and clinked it against hers, and they smiled at each other.

Their pizza arrived, and his looked delicious.

"Mine's more colorful than yours," he said. "How about that?"

She rolled her eyes. "It's not all about *color*."

"I like colorful things. Not poison dart frogs, but your vest, for example. Very colorful."

She looked down. "Is it too much?"

"No, it's perfect." He bit into his pizza, careful to take a bite with both prosciutto and grilled pineapple. "Mmm, that's just perfect, too."

"I'll take your word for it. I'll be over here with my uncolorful pizza."

They did not trade slices of pizza this time.

But afterward, they took an Uber to Treatzz, where they each got a bubble waffle with two scoops of ice cream, and they tried each other's flavors.

"I'm glad you didn't get the olive oil," he said. "Olive oil doesn't belong in ice cream."

"I agree."

"Wow! We agree on something!" he said with exaggerated shock. "I might not have been able to kiss you afterward if you'd had olive oil ice cream."

She bumped his shoulder as they walked up Ossington. "Oh, come on. You would have kissed me."

He pretended to seriously think on this. "You're right," he said quietly. "I would have kissed you."

He held a napkin up to her mouth and wiped a drop of melted lemon meringue ice cream away. Their faces were so close together now, and for a moment, he had to stop walking, transfixed by her mouth.

And then she did something truly naughty.

She bit her lower lip, just the way he'd taught her. Slowly, deliberately.

His pants felt a bit tight.

"Mike," she said, "you should probably eat your ice cream so it doesn't keep dripping."

He looked down and saw a drop of chocolate ginger ice cream on the sidewalk.

"That's a travesty," he murmured. "It's all your fault for distracting me."

She rolled her eyes.

How could a woman look so cute when she rolled her eyes? It was unfair.

He didn't look cute when *he* rolled his eyes.

"Can I try your fig goat cheese?" he asked. "I don't think goat cheese belongs in ice cream, either, but since it's your favorite, I'm curious."

She held her bubble waffle away from him, curling her hands around it protectively.

"Come on." He smiled. "I'll give you an orgasm."

"You'll give me an orgasm anyway."

Well, busted.

He stroked a thumb over her jaw—he'd learned she particularly like that spot.

"You play dirty." She held her cone-shaped bubble waffle toward him.

The fig goat cheese ice cream wasn't as good as the chocolate ginger but not as weird as he'd expected.

"Admit it," she said. "You want to eat it every damn day."

"No, I want to eat you every damn day."

She burst into laughter.

Okay, maybe his delivery needed a little work, but they were having fun.

They walked toward his apartment, and once they were done their ice cream, he got to hold her hand.

Why had he avoided dating for so long? It wasn't that hard.

While waiting for a stoplight, he kissed that spot on her jaw again, and the way she arched her neck as she told him, once more, that he played dirty, was lovely.

He wished they weren't still ten minutes away from home.

As soon as they were inside the door of his apartment, they slipped off their shoes, and he came up behind her and wrapped his arms around her waist. He swayed his hips.

"See, we're dancing," he said.

To his surprise, she didn't protest; instead, she leaned back against him and shut her eyes. He figured they should have some music, so he started humming "Beauty and the Beast."

Her eyes flew open. "Oh, God. Did you hear me singing in your shower last weekend?"

He switched to humming "Gaston."

"Oh, no," she said. "I thought I was quiet. I never sing in front of anyone."

"Why not? You have a nice voice."

"I'm not sure I'll be able to look you in the eye again, now that I know you heard me."

"That's okay. I'm flexible. You don't have to look at me."

He continued to sway his hips as he began kissing her neck. His hands roamed over her body, cupping her breasts through her clothing. He caressed her nipple at the same time as he lightly bit her neck.

She squirmed against him, her ass pressing against his cock.

"I love the preppy look you've got going on today," he said. "Too bad I have to ruin it."

He pulled her vest and shirt over her head in one move, then undid her bra.

"Yes," he murmured, "you're so beautiful, Charlotte. I can't believe I get to touch you."

"Then touch me. Now."

He chuckled as he flicked his thumb over her nipple again, but this time, there were no clothes in the way. He nuzzled the base of her neck and squeezed her breast.

"Is this how you want me to touch you?" he asked.

"Yes, and…"

He opened the button on her jeans with one hand. He was still standing behind her, his body pressed against hers, as he slid his hand inside her jeans, but over top of her underwear.

"Like this?"

"Not quite." She looked back at him. "You're really damn infuriating, you know."

He laughed softly. "Show me what you want."

She guided his hand inside her panties, and they both groaned as he stroked her wet folds. His cock was rock hard, but he paid it no attention as he slipped his fingers over her entrance and pressed one inside. He couldn't get very deep, due to the angle when he was behind her, but she gasped all the same.

He slid his finger in and out of her as he stroked her clit with his thumb, planting kisses up and down her neck. When he massaged her breast in his other hand, she jerked against him.

He paused for a moment. "Good?"

"Keep going, you idiot."

"Tsk-tsk. That's no way to talk to the man who's bringing you untold pleasure."

"Untold pleasure? You sure have a high opinion of your…self."

She'd lost her ability to talk clearly, and he smirked.

When he circled her clit the next time, she stiffened in his arms and clenched around his fingers.

"Oh my God." She collapsed back against him.

He carried her to bed and rolled her onto her stomach once

he'd removed the rest of her clothes. She was so lovely to look at. Naked. In his bed.

He made quick work of his own clothes, rolled on a condom, then rubbed the tip of his cock over her entrance. She moaned in frustration until he slid inside her from behind.

Yes. This felt good. Right.

He wasn't the most experienced in the bedroom, no. But somehow, she responded to everything he did. Somehow, he was capable of making her feel good, and that was what mattered.

She gripped the pillow in her hands, and then she turned her head so she could kiss him.

Her lips on his. When he was buried deep inside her.

He licked his finger and brought it between her legs. It took a moment to find her clit when she kept bucking her hips against him, but he could tell when she suddenly stilled and made a soft mewl.

He circled her clit as he thrust in and out of her, planting kisses wherever he could.

When she tensed around him and cried out, she pulled him over the edge.

He grinned as he held her afterward, because this was utterly, utterly real, and it was more amazing than anything he'd dared to imagine.

The next morning, there were no spiders on the wall, so Mike didn't ruin the mood by shrieking. Instead, he and Charlotte sleepily cuddled before he slid inside her.

And then, when she was sated from what sounded like two pretty spectacular orgasms—he couldn't help feeling mighty pleased with himself—he pulled a small package out of his night table and handed it to her.

"You got me a present? Already?" she asked.

"Just something small."

Or did taking it slow mean you weren't supposed to give each other presents?

Ugh, he didn't know these things, but he *did* know of a little store nearby that sold stuff he thought she'd like.

"In honor of our first real date," he said, trying to sound like it was no big deal.

She was already tearing open the wrapping paper. She pulled out a set of washi tapes. One had a night sky, nearly black with golden stars and a crescent moon. Another had flowers. The third had toadstools—presumably not the poisonous variety.

"These are really cute." She turned them around in her hand, then set them aside and picked up the stickers. Rather than sticker sheets, they were in a little plastic bag. She opened it up and looked at the nature stickers. Trees and flowers and such.

"For your day planner," he explained.

"You're the only who's seen the inside of that day planner. Other than me, obviously."

"You don't want anyone to know that you like cute stickers?"

She shrugged, then kissed him on the lips. "Thanks, Mike. Nobody's ever gotten me a gift like this before. You're great."

Though he felt awkward, he breathed out a sigh of relief.

It wasn't just her words. It was the way she looked at him, the sincerity of it. Charlotte could be flippant sometimes, but not now.

He swallowed and turned away. "Um, right. I guess I should make you some coffee."

She grabbed his hand before he could get up. "You're bad at receiving compliments. I never realized."

"It's uncomfortable." He swallowed again. "When you're constantly told you're shit and will never amount to anything, you get used to that. You keep expecting to fuck up, and you don't believe any good things people say about you."

He wasn't usually quite so bad at it anymore, and if he needed to, he'd laugh and smile and change the topic.

But he wasn't able to do that now. And all those things that he'd been told for years…they started to crowd his head again, in new and twisted ways.

This is what happens when you try to get close to anyone. How do you think you can have a relationship when you can't even take a fucking compliment? You're such a screw-up.

He clenched his hand and tried to silence his brain.

"Hey." Charlotte's hand was on his leg, grounding him.

Oh, God. She was seeing him like this, being all weird.

"It's okay," she said. "I don't have to say nice things right now, even if they're true. I can express my continued dismay that you ordered *posh* Hawaiian pizza last night. I mean, really, Mike? Pineapple on pizza? Are you for real?" She lightly smacked him on the shoulder. "Time for you to make me some coffee, and no damn decaf."

She always knew the right things to say.

By the time they were having breakfast and Charlotte was on her third cup of coffee—geez, that woman could really knock back her coffee—Mike was feeling like himself again.

But he didn't want Charlotte to leave.

"How about we extend our first date?" he said. "Let's go to the island."

She looked at him in horror. "You know how I feel about spontaneity and unplanned social interaction."

"No, I don't believe you've ever told me before."

"Take an educated guess."

He shrugged and spent a moment admiring her. She'd put on her clothes from yesterday. They were slightly rumpled, but she looked cute with her face scrunched up like that.

"So," she said, "you want to take the ferry to the island? Walk around, go to the amusement park? Have fun?" She sounded awful cranky about the whole thing, but there was a glimmer in her eye.

"Yeah. I'll buy you as many coffees as you need to get through the day."

"I have plans with my friends tonight, so we'll have to be back by eight."

"No problem. I can't wait to see you on a swan boat, eating cotton candy."

"I'm not riding a fucking swan boat," she said, though he had a feeling he could convince her. "But fine, we can go."

"You are such a softy and a pushover."

"Shh. That's secret information." She squeezed his hand.

[17]

ONCE AGAIN, Charlotte was the first one to arrive at Ossington Cider Bar, and once again, there were no tables for five available, so she waited at the bar. She ordered a glass of dry, musty cider and smiled as she imagined Mike teasing her about it.

After hanging out with him for twenty-four hours, it was nice to have a few moments to herself. Sure, she was surrounded by people, but none of them were paying attention to her.

Admittedly, being with Mike wasn't as draining as being with other people. She could spend lots of time with him without getting stabby, and when she wanted a few minutes of quiet, he was happy to oblige and simply hold her hand.

Though she still hadn't forgiven him for taking her on the log flume ride at Centreville. He'd insisted it would be lots of fun.

She'd gotten fucking *soaked*.

Somehow, she'd ended up getting twice as wet as he had. How unfair.

But they'd laughed afterward, and she supposed it hadn't been *that* bad, given the hot weather. When she'd refused cotton candy, he'd bought her a coffee as a consolation prize.

He'd also dragged her onto the swan ride and convinced her

to rent a tandem bicycle so they could bike around the Toronto Islands. There were multiple islands, many connected by short bridges, and they'd ridden past the houses on Algonquin and Ward's Islands—it could be cool to live there, she supposed.

So, yes, apparently being spontaneous could be tolerable at times.

It was different from how it had been with Brad. Mike would only nudge her a little out of her comfort zone, and he would respect her if she refused to do something. He clearly understood who she was. Whereas Brad hadn't understood her at all and had kept pushing her to do things she absolutely hated.

Also, Mike didn't steal the blankets in his sleep or talk too loudly. He did hate spiders, which were noble creatures in her opinion, but somehow, that didn't bother her.

"Hey!" Nicole said, coming up beside Charlotte. "How was your first real date last night?"

"It was good. I stayed over and we went to the island today. Even went on the swan ride."

"You did *what*?"

Charlotte shrugged. "He's very persuasive."

"What did he do to persuade you?" Nicole waggled her eyebrows.

"Not telling."

"I'll assume it was very dirty."

"You can assume whatever you want."

"Is there photographic evidence of you in the swan boat?"

"Um, no," Charlotte said, though it was a lie. The photographic evidence was, however, on Mike's phone.

Sierra walked over. "What's this about Charlotte and a swan?"

"She and Mike went on the swan ride at Centreville."

"No! She didn't!"

"Ah, so you're still dating Mike Guo." Julie walked over to them, a tray of empty glasses in her hands. "This is getting serious."

Dear God. Charlotte hung her head.

See what happened when you went on a fucking swan ride with a cute guy?

"Mom and Dad are going to be so pleased," Julie said, then made a face. "Dammit, they really are going to be pleased."

"Don't you dare tell—"

"Who, me? I would never."

"Right."

"What's Mike been doing for the last two decades anyway?" Julie asked.

"He's a financial advisor now," Charlotte said.

"How boring."

Charlotte shot her sister a death glare. The death glare she'd specifically perfected for use with Julie.

"What else has he been up to?" Julie asked, unperturbed.

Getting hot.

Julie pointed at her. "You look like you're daydreaming about him."

"Am not."

"Julie's right," Nicole said.

Charlotte aimed her death glare at Nicole, but Nicole seemed equally unperturbed.

Dammit, she was losing her touch.

"Anyway, as much as I'd love to stay and chat," Julie said, "I think your table is ready."

Sierra, Nicole, and Charlotte followed the hostess to the back patio and took their seats.

"You're practically glowing," Nicole said to Charlotte.

"Fuck off," Charlotte said.

"No, really, you are. I'm happy for you."

"Are you? I thought you didn't do relationships."

"That doesn't mean I can't be happy for my friends. As long as he treats you right and doesn't propose to you at a baseball game or swallow your identity."

Yeah, Charlotte knew that was what Nicole feared, due to past experience.

Nicole had been with her ex for a couple of years when he suggested they open up their relationship, which resulted in her having lots of fun with other guys, and him whining about not getting any action. She'd realized just how good sex could be and also how much of herself she'd changed for him. So, she'd ended it.

But Charlotte didn't feel like she was losing her individual identity in her relationship, even if Mike was getting her to do things she wouldn't normally do, and she was very happy with the sex. She still felt like herself, just with more sex and spontaneity. And, okay, sometimes she was less ornery when she was with him.

"Are you bringing him to Amy's wedding?" Sierra asked.

"Yes, he's agreed to come."

"Are you going to dance with him?"

"Don't be ridiculous. He can dance by himself."

Knowing Mike, he'd probably ask her to dance once or twice, but then he'd let it go. He wouldn't use his powers of persuasion, knowing that she detested dancing more than swan rides and sweet cider.

Amy sat down across from her. "How was your date?"

"Apparently it was awesome," Sierra said. "She keeps trying not to smile."

"Where's Rose?" Charlotte asked, rather than answering Amy's question.

"Oh." Nicole frowned. "She's not feeling well today."

"Is she sick?" Amy asked. "I'll bring her some soup."

Charlotte, Nicole, and Sierra all looked at each other. Amy was new to their group, and she didn't know everything about Rose. Charlotte wasn't going to be the one who told Amy the truth, not without Rose's permission.

Because if Rose wasn't up to hanging out tonight, Charlotte

was pretty sure of the reason. She made a mental note to text her friend tomorrow.

"Rose is just tired," Nicole said. "Didn't have a good night's sleep." Which was probably true. "But I'm sure she's sad that she's missing this exciting discussion of Charlotte's new *boyfriend*."

Charlotte sighed and looked down at her menu.

And then, because she couldn't seem to help herself, she thought of the way Mike had slid his hands all over her body last night as he held her from behind, and that cheeky smile he'd given her after she'd gotten soaked from the flume ride.

Is that a picture of you on a swan boat? Rose asked.

Yes, Charlotte texted. Mike had sent it to her earlier, and she hoped it would give her friend a laugh. *But please don't send it to anyone else. For your eyes only.*

Oh, don't worry, I would NEVER do something like that...

Charlotte wasn't an expert at discerning people's moods from text messages, but it did seem like Rose was doing okay, if she was making jokes.

How are you? Charlotte asked.

Better than yesterday. I actually slept last night. Only four hours, but it's better than nothing, and I don't feel quite as depressed.

Rose had struggled with depression for as long as Charlotte had known her. It ran in Rose's family.

You know, Rose said, *I think it would be better for my mental health if I lived with someone. Not you, don't worry. Sierra, maybe, once Amy gets married. You think I should ask?*

Charlotte definitely didn't want to live with a friend, but not everyone in the world was like her, thank God. Society would be completely dysfunctional if that were the case.

Well, maybe it already was. But still.

Sure, why not? she said to Rose. *Worst thing that could happen is she says no.*

Though Rose might take that harder than Charlotte would.

I don't want to be a burden, Rose said.

I'm sure you're not a burden to live with. Not that Charlotte knew from personal experience. She'd lived with Nicole and Sierra for three years in undergrad, but Rose had lived with someone else during university. However, Rose was always hyper-aware of not causing problems for other people.

It's not like I want someone to look after me, Rose said. *I just want the company. To eat dinner with another person sometimes, you know?*

You should ask her.

Okay, I will. I'm heading out now to get some fresh air.

Sounds awful.

Going on walks is good for you!

So you've told me, Charlotte said.

Thank you. For the swan boat picture. I'll be sure to plaster it all over social media.

You're hilarious.

[18]

Tuesday afternoon, Charlotte looked at the Marquardt inversion she'd run on a section of airborne EM data and swore. She'd have to play with the settings tomorrow because the result wasn't fitting the data well enough. But for now, she was finished work.

Time to do some research on relationships so she didn't fuck things up with Mike. She made a list of popular relationship advice columns and forums then set about reading them.

An hour later, she was a jittery mess.

Okay, maybe doing a little light research on the internet when it came to dating and relationships wasn't the best idea. She should have learned that lesson after the research she'd done prior to her first practice date.

Because now she was petrified of all the ways her relationship could go wrong. There were so many things she simply hadn't considered.

For example, he could have a collection of creepy porcelain dolls that he insisted on displaying in his living room.

Charlotte wasn't disturbed by much, but that was fucking scary.

Fortunately, she'd been to Mike's apartment, and he did not

have such a collection, although she hadn't looked in his bedroom closet. She should do that next time.

Another possibility was that he could throw out all her clothes and replace them with a wardrobe *he* deemed appropriate. Like a closet full of dresses with no pajama pants in sight.

Or he could be cheating on her with her best friend.

Or the nanny.

Or their scuba instructor.

He could spend half their savings on exotic pets or an over-the-top "man cave" while getting mad when she dared to spend money on a pedicure.

He could become ridiculously insecure if she made more money than him.

Or he could get pissed off because she wanted him to look after their baby for half an hour while she relaxed in the bath, after having literally no time to herself for a month.

Or he could throw her a surprise party after she told him, repeatedly, that she hated surprise parties, then get mad when she spent fifteen minutes hiding in the washroom.

No, the last one would never happen. That was something Brad might have done, but Mike would never.

There were so many horror stories that she couldn't see applying to Mike, but was she naïve? Many men hid certain parts of themselves at the beginning.

He might not do anything as awful as cheating on her with the scuba instructor, but there were tons of less dramatic possibilities. She felt terribly unprepared.

Oh, God. Why was she in a relationship? It was so much easier to be alone.

And why was her lower back hurting?

She looked at the calendar and swore.

~

An hour later, Charlotte was curled up on her couch with a hot water bottle, and the ibuprofen was taking the edge off her cramps, but she still felt like shit.

When her phone buzzed, she practically screamed.

It was just Mike, though, asking if she wanted to do something tonight.

What if he wanted to show her his creepy doll collection?

A few minutes later, he texted her again. *I'm going to the grocery store after leaving the office. I could make us dinner?*

Okay, so it had nothing to do with his creepy doll collection.

Or was dinner just a ruse?

Sorry, she texted. *Not in the mood to leave my apartment.* She hesitated. She and Mike had only been on one proper date, as well as a handful of fake ones. Was it too soon to tell him the truth? Was he one of those guys who was totally disgusted by periods and would flip out if he had to see or—God forbid—buy a package of unopened pads or tampons? She'd read about at least two such men this afternoon, plus another who was in desperate need of basic biology lessons.

Better to find out sooner rather than later.

It's a bad time of month, she added. *I have cramps.*

She was also bleeding heavily and wearing an overnight pad even though it wasn't bedtime, but he didn't need to know *that* much.

He replied quickly. *I could bring the food to your apartment and cook there? No Hawaiian pizza, I promise.*

Someone else cooking for her, and she didn't even need to leave home?

Sure, she replied.

Do you need anything from the pharmacy? Painkillers? Other supplies?

He was willing to buy whatever she needed. It was a small thing, but still.

No, I have everything, she texted. *See you soon.*

She settled on her couch and started watching a crime show. She was on her second episode and had just poured more water into her hot water bottle when her phone rang.

But it wasn't Mike asking to be buzzed in. It was her parents calling.

"Charlotte," Dad said. "How are you? Have you found any gold deposits?"

"I'm doing okay."

"You're not coming home for the Labor Day weekend? Your mother said you have a wedding."

"Wah, who has a wedding on a long weekend?" Mom asked, since of course this conversation was on speakerphone. "Don't they know you have parents to visit?"

"Mom, the wedding isn't about me," Charlotte said.

"But other people must have families to visit, too."

"It's better for Victor's family, okay? They're out west and will be flying in. This way, they can have more time in Toronto without missing work. And venues fill up quickly. There weren't a ton of options."

"Who's Victor?"

Charlotte thought that had been obvious. "The groom."

"Oh, yes. I remember now. Why can't you be like Amy and meet a nice young man?"

"Victor is forty and covered in tattoos." She was fond of Victor in a plutonic/platonic way, but she didn't think he was quite what her parents had imagined.

But there was only a second's hesitation before her mother said, "This is not a problem."

Clearly, her parents were getting desperate to marry her off.

She wasn't ready to tell them about Mike. Another month or two. She was definitely unprepared to deal with her mother's excitement and questions.

"Look, Mom, I'm having cramps right now."

"Ah, that's too bad. I will talk to you later, but we want to know if we could visit next weekend, since you cannot visit us for Labor Day. We can come to Toronto and go shopping."

"We've been through this before. I'm not going shopping with you. I don't have the fortitude for that."

"Why are you using such big words? And shopping with me is not a hardship. I find you great clothes!"

No, Mom would find clothes that were not her style and not the most comfortable for sitting around her apartment all day.

Although now that Charlotte was going out more often, perhaps she needed more clothing to wear in public…

Nope. She shot down that idea immediately.

Buying clothes was an unfortunate necessity, but shopping with Nicole was preferable to shopping with Mom. At least her friend had good taste and wouldn't try to convince her to buy something awful. Shopping with her mother was super exhausting.

"Fine," Mom huffed. "We can come for lunch with you and Julie next Saturday?"

"Sure, but Amy's bachelorette party is in the evening. I'll have to go by five."

"We will be heading back to Ashton Corners by then. No problem."

Charlotte talked to her parents for a little longer, then made a list of all the shitty things that a boyfriend could do, based on her earlier research.

Hopefully the day would improve from here.

When Mike walked into her apartment with a couple bags of groceries, Charlotte kissed him on the lips, then returned to the couch and curled up with her hot water bottle.

"How are you doing now?" he asked, coming to sit beside her.

"Better." She seemed to have instantly improved with his

company. Just, like, twenty-five percent, but it was still something. "What are you making for dinner?"

"Spaghetti with meatballs. The meatballs aren't homemade, so don't be too impressed."

"I don't care, as long as I don't have to think about cooking."

"We're also having roasted vegetables on the side."

"Fancy." She hoped that didn't sound sarcastic, but sarcasm had a tendency to creep into her voice at times.

"You need anything?" he asked. "Tea? Coffee?"

"Coffee. Always coffee." She'd once read that caffeine could make cramps worse, but that hadn't been her experience.

Five minutes later, he set down her French press and her *Schist Happens* mug on the coffee table. He even made a point of using the coasters.

"I'll cook now," he said. "You just relax."

She snuggled up on the couch and started her crime show again. It seemed like such a luxury to lie back and relax while someone else made dinner in her kitchen. She felt almost guilty but told herself not to.

She'd just finished an episode when Mike said, "Dinner's ready."

She shuffled over to the small dining room table. There were two plates of spaghetti with tomato sauce and meatballs, plus roasted eggplant, zucchini, and red pepper. It was a sign of how crappy she felt that she didn't even bother making a comment about the eggplant.

But wait. She smelled something that wasn't food.

"You got me flowers?" she asked incredulously. Somehow, she'd failed to notice this when he entered her apartment. Probably because she was in pain.

"Why not? You didn't have a vase, so I had to use an empty wine bottle."

She was hardly an expert on flowers, but these looked like dahlias. And yes, she sounded cranky, but she did like them.

When Mike sat down across from her and set the parmesan on the table, she helped herself to a generous amount of cheese, as well as black pepper—she loved black pepper on everything. She speared a meatball and popped it in her mouth.

"My compliments to whoever produced these meatballs," she said.

He smiled at her.

"And thank you…for everything. It's been a long time since anyone did something like this for me." She gestured to the flowers and food.

Charlotte felt awkward giving compliments, and Mike, once again, looked awkward receiving a compliment.

"It's nothing," he said.

"It's not nothing. Like I said, it's been a while since anyone did this for me."

"Then people are idiots."

"Oh, come on. I might have sworn off dating for five years, but I'm also a cranky pain in the ass who spends her time drinking coffee, swearing at the computer, and wearing pajamas—"

"—and a T-shirt with the word 'cummingtonite,' which intrigues me."

Dear God, was that what she was wearing today?

She looked down. Yep. A black shirt that said *Cummingtonite?* followed by a chemical formula.

"It's a mineral," she said.

"Uh-huh."

"Named after Cummington, Massachusetts."

"Sounds like a made-up place," he said.

"I swear, it's real."

"Don't worry, I believe you."

"You sound skeptical."

"I'm not."

"You're doing that annoying skeptical voice again." She sighed. "See, this is why I don't understand why you put up with me."

"It sounds like you're fishing for compliments."

"How dare you."

She was unfit to be in a relationship. He'd made her a nice meal and now she was trying to argue about stupid shit.

He reached across the table and took her hand. "I like being with you, truly. I like arguing with you, and you look cute when you're riled up."

"I do not."

"See how hard it can be to accept a compliment?"

The pair of them. Did they have any idea what they were doing?

But he was sweet and easy to be with. He cooked dinner and made her coffee, and he'd yet to throw her a surprise party or cheat on her with a scuba instructor. She really did want to give this a go.

It was just a little hard to believe he wanted to be with her at times.

Or maybe that was her menstrual cramps talking.

After dinner, she discovered he'd brought her chocolate cake. *Triple* chocolate cake. He made her more coffee to have with dessert, and they watched a movie. He didn't do anything annoying like talk during the movie, just held her against him and absently stroked her shoulder, which was more distracting than it should have been.

This was exactly what she wanted from a relationship.

Later, she had a shower and he made her another hot water bottle.

"Do you want me to stay?" he asked.

She did, but… "I'm not going to be in the mood tonight."

"I don't have to stay only when we have sex."

"You should know that I never want to have sex in the first three days of my period. Even when ibuprofen has sufficiently dulled my cramps, I bleed heavily, and I'm just not into it. After the third day, though, if you don't mind putting down a towel…"

Ugh, was she sharing too much information on bodily functions?

He just nodded. "Okay."

They climbed into bed at ten—early for her—and he simply held her.

"If this is what's going to happen every month," she said, "then I won't mind getting my period so much."

His chuckle vibrated through her. "If this is what you want each month, I can arrange it."

"I hated going to the office when I had cramps. That's one of the nice things about working from home. If I need to take the afternoon off, I can. No one will question me. Or my hot water bottle. Though going to the office was better than my geology field course." She shuddered. "If I'd known about that, maybe I would have picked another type of engineering."

"What did your field course involve?"

"I looked at my schedule at the beginning of second year and saw a five-hour lab, and I thought it had to be an exaggeration. But, no. They loaded us into a school bus and took us to outcrops in the area to study different types of rocks. Thirty kids wearing hard hats—even when the rocks were only up to our hip—at the side of the road, holding compasses and looking like idiots. Sometimes it took more than five hours. You have no access to a washroom during that time, and twice, I'd just gotten my period. It was awful."

And a fucking mess.

She was just thankful she'd never passed out on the side of the road.

She'd tried taking the pill—a couple different ones—but hated the side effects. They made her weepy and even more irritable. Plus, they killed her libido. Though it might be worth trying another. It would be fantastic if she could find something that worked for her.

"Luckily," she said, "I didn't have my period for field school at the end of second year. That was two weeks long, so it was very lucky. I can't imagine doing field work. Like, collecting some of the data I interpret. Not for me. Instead, I just sit around my apartment without proper pants."

"I'm certainly not complaining."

"You can complain about the fact that I spent ten minutes talking about periods."

"Nah. I get to spend time with you. It's all good."

It seemed like a miracle that Mike was still here. That he'd found her again, twenty years later. That they were together like this, after she'd made that ridiculous you-can-teach-me-how-to-date proposal.

They were two people who'd struggled with relationships, who were lacking experience, yet here they were…and they both seemed to have trouble believing it was real.

She was getting far too sappy.

He'd been spooning her, but now she turned over and kissed him on the lips. He cupped her cheek and took his time, and even though she still felt crappy, that kiss seemed to travel all the way down to her toes, filling every jagged crevice inside her. Like magma filling the fractures in a rock, then solidifying.

She wanted to hear him say again that no, he didn't find her too much of a pain in the ass, but she wasn't going to ask.

She was just going to lie here with him and enjoy it.

Eventually, he turned out the light, and unlike on the weekend, when they'd moved to opposite sides of the bed to sleep, he held her. Though she never thought she'd be able to fall asleep while cuddling, she figured she probably could now.

She did, indeed, fall asleep in his arms.

And that night, she dreamed of triple chocolate cake.

[19]

On Thursday, Mike took Charlotte to an Ethiopian restaurant near Ossington and Bloor for dinner.

It was good to see her again. She looked better than she had two days ago, when she'd been pale and clearly in pain. Not that she hadn't still been beautiful, but he hated to see her unwell. It caused his chest to tighten.

The server set a large platter in front of them, with several piles of food on the injera. Mike couldn't identify everything, but there were a couple with meat, one of which was doro wat, and several vegetarian items. One looked like lentils; another looked like collard greens. In the center of the platter was some salad. There was also a plate with more injera, and Mike tore off a piece and used it to scoop up the lentils.

Yes, it was as good as he remembered.

And this time, Charlotte was with him.

At the end of the meal, they cleaned their hands with wet wipes, and he suggested they do the coffee ceremony. The coffee came with a big dish of popcorn. He and Charlotte eyed it, then looked at each other and laughed.

"I'm not sure I could possibly eat more," she said.

She still ate a few handfuls.

All the food did not, of course, prevent her from drinking lots of coffee. He only had a small amount, since it was almost eight and he had to work tomorrow.

When he said she could have the rest, she grinned and said, "I love you."

He immediately stiffened, and she did, too, looking horrified that she'd said those words.

"I didn't mean it…like that," she stammered. "I was just talking about the coffee. I love that you're letting me have more than my share of coffee. You know what I mean."

Yeah, he did.

But he didn't think anyone had ever said those words to him before, and this hadn't been real. It had just been about coffee.

You think anyone could ever love you? Ha!

He grimaced.

"Shit, Mike, I'm sorry," she said. "I'm never able to love people this quickly. It's not about *you*. It's too soon. We had our first real date less than a week ago."

"I know," he said, irritated with himself.

"Do you want to, um, talk about it?" She sounded uncomfortable with the idea, but he knew she was sincere.

"Not here."

As they headed back to her apartment, he tried to put on a cheerful façade, but it was hard when all these stupid thoughts were rolling around in his brain.

Once they were inside, she pulled off her bra through her sleeve and put on a pair of pajama shorts. She made herself a hot water bottle before climbing into bed; he took off his jeans and got in with her.

"What's up?" she asked.

This was the thing about relationships. People were supposed to *know* stuff about you.

"Sometimes," he said, "people tell others, 'I'm sure your

parents love you,' but I'm convinced my parents didn't love me and Angela. I used to think that if only I was good enough, they'd love me, but I was a constant disappointment, always getting in trouble for minor things. All of grade seven and eight, my room didn't have a door on it and half my stuff was thrown out. More than once, they made me sleep in the garage. They were always yelling, asking us if we ever thought about what we were doing to them, like we were responsible for their unhappiness, and..."

For a minute, he was back in that house in Ashton Corners, the one he tried to forget.

"Maybe some people in town wouldn't have considered your parents normal, either," he continued. "You'd build a cool Lego structure, and your parents would talk about how you were so smart, you would get a scholarship to a good engineering school. You were only six, but they talked about university scholarships. Whereas mine would get mad when I didn't draw what they told me to draw, then take all the money from my piggybank and tell me I was an embarrassment." He paused. "If it hadn't been for your family, I probably would have hated being Asian. I would have assumed that's why my parents were the way they were, since that was the big difference between me and nearly every kid at school. School made me anxious, because I worried about what my parents would do if I didn't get a perfect grade, but people seemed to like me at school. I made myself easy to like. Anyway..." That was enough for now. Relationships were supposed to be happy things, weren't they?

But before he could comment on something else, she said, "What happened after you moved?" She hesitated. "You don't have to tell me much, if you don't want."

"My parents claimed we had to be in the Toronto area if Angela and I had any hope of going to university. Because clearly we were too stupid to live away from our family, and there are multiple schools in the GTA."

"Your parents were such *turds.*"

He chuckled, but then he said, "Yeah. They were emotionally abusive." He paused. "In high school and university, I didn't date. Whenever I started to get close to someone, I'd freak out and distance myself, because I worried that I'd make them miserable, or they'd realize I was a piece of shit. Angela, on the other hand, craved the approval she couldn't get at home, and she had a string of shitty relationships, the last one being her marriage when she was twenty. She got pregnant right after she finished university. My parents were furious with her for getting pregnant so young…and then my mom made the pregnancy all about her being a grandma for the first time. Threw a baby shower Angela didn't want, tried to force herself into the delivery room when Angela made it clear she didn't want her there. Blamed Bailey's slightly low birth weight on Angela. Mocked her for not immediately losing all the baby weight. Told her that postpartum depression was bullshit. Stopped by without warning multiple times a week."

He trailed off, thinking back to those awful days. He would defend his sister and try to deflect attention from Angela and Bailey to him. He was still living with his parents, even though he was miserable. Yet, although his mother and father thought he was incompetent, they expected him to look after them as they grew old. They laid on the guilt. He wouldn't want his poor parents to suffer, would he? What would people think?

"That stuff with Angela made me have a breakdown," he said. "I realized how messed up everything was, though it's hard to fully comprehend when that's all you've ever known."

He'd never spent much time at other friends' houses, and of course their families might act differently when he was around. Mike's parents were different in public, that was for sure.

"I remembered your family," he said quietly. "I told myself they never would have behaved quite like that. I got a therapist. I moved out, went no contact with my parents, though it made me feel incredibly guilty at first. Helped Angela leave her husband.

And things did get better. In fact, I was amazed by what I was able to accomplish. I'd been led to believe I could do, well, nothing, and would only end up disappointing people."

"Jesus, Mike," Charlotte said. "I had no idea. They were so wrong about you."

"Yeah, so wrong." He tried to say it with conviction, but his voice wobbled.

There had been so much he'd had to unlearn, and it was still hard to believe in himself at times. He'd feel like he was a walking fraud, and if anyone got too close and peeled back the layers, they'd find nothing underneath.

But he also had lots of practice telling himself that wasn't true.

"At first," he said, "I was in no place to be in a relationship. After years of therapy, I was much better, but that one thing was still a bit hard. Which is why I thought practice dating would be good for me."

"Do you go to therapy anymore?"

"Not for a few years, but maybe I should start again. I still have a little baggage, and I don't want to fuck things up with you. Also, I think I'd like to have kids one day, and I don't want to fuck up being a parent, either." He paused. "Do you want kids?"

Now he felt like he was fucking up again. Talking about kids with someone whom he'd been dating for such a short period of time—surely that was going too fast?

Though it had seemed natural to ask, and it was good to know these things early on, right?

"I think so," she said. "It's part of the reason I wanted to start dating again. Beneath the cranky hermit exterior, I've dreamed of weddings—small ones, with no dancing—since I was little, and wanted children to wreak havoc on my life." She smiled as she spoke. "The only problem is that I don't think you're supposed to have much caffeine when you're pregnant and..." She made a face. "Obviously, that would be hard for me."

"We're not doing a great job of taking this slow."

"We're not. Screw you, being so sweet and bringing me fucking flowers and chocolate cake and letting me have most of the coffee. You're too goddamn thoughtful." She lightly shoved his shoulder. "Is it better if I compliment you using swear words? Does that make it easier?"

"I do really like you, Charlotte. And yeah, maybe a little."

"Your parents are toxic assholes, and you've done a lot of work to heal yourself. I'm proud of you. You turned out so well in spite of them."

He swallowed. "Now don't go overboard on the compliments."

"Do they ever try to contact you?"

"They did at one point, but I moved and changed my number, and my aunt and uncle started blackmailing them."

"Blackmailing them? With what?"

"I'm not sure, but they seem to believe it would be enough to put my parents in prison."

Charlotte's eyes widened.

"Financial stuff, I assume," he said. "It was never clear how my parents got all their money, and I try not to think about it. My aunt and uncle had very little to do with my family when we were younger because they couldn't stand my parents. But they—and my cousins—talk to me and Angela. They live far away, though."

"And you and Angela?"

"We get along okay, but it's tough. Seeing each other makes us remember our childhood, and we were taught to compete, so sometimes we bring out the worst in each other. Plus, we both thought the other had it easier. She moved away from Toronto, and I think that's worked out best for her and Bailey."

Charlotte used some choice swear words to describe his parents again, then rolled him over so she could hold him from behind, similar to how he'd held her on Tuesday night.

"You can be the little spoon," she said.

"It's called jetpacking."

"What?"

"I'm not sure where I heard it, but when the smaller person is on the outside, it's like they're a jetpack on the other person's back. Hence the term."

"Ah. I'm making you powerful. Got it."

Yeah, you kind of are.

"You have shit taste," she said, "in cider and pizza—"

"Hey!"

"—and you don't appreciate spiders, but other than that, you're pretty wonderful. Wait. I thought of another flaw."

"And what's that?" he asked.

"You drink decaf lattes sometimes."

"Oh, come on. Not everyone needs ten servings of caffeine a day."

"And sometimes, you wear too many clothes."

"Charlotte…"

He knocked off his jetpack, turned over, and started tickling her. He didn't know where she was most ticklish, but this, he figured, was one of the many things you got to learn about someone when you were in a relationship.

When she tried to tickle his nipples—damn her—he rolled her underneath him and pinned her wrists above her head.

She was gasping for breath and her cheeks were a delightful rosy color.

"Another flaw," she said. "You play dirty in tickle fights."

"It's a better flaw than being offended by pineapple on pizza."

"For fuck's sake."

And then he had to kiss her.

When he came up for air, she touched his cheek and said, without any mischief in her voice this time, "I'm glad my first relationship in five years is with you."

Yes, he'd have to get used to compliments from Charlotte.

[20]

ALTHOUGH THE RESTAURANT was called Congee Princess, Charlotte's family hadn't ordered any congee. Nor had any of the nearby tables, from what she could see. There was, of course, a whole page of congee in the menu, but the menu was as thick as a book.

She and Julie had let their parents order, as usual, and now their table was weighed down with massive amounts of food. Seafood chow mein. Fried eggplant with minced pork. Fried bean curd with vegetables. Scallops. Duck.

The server put a plate of vegetables with oyster sauce on their table. Fried rice appeared a moment later.

"You always order too much," Julie said.

Mom clucked her tongue. "I make sure you have leftovers. I am a thoughtful mother! You are too skinny. Not eating enough." She served Julie some bean curd.

"You know I don't like that. You only order it because it's Charlotte's favorite."

Charlotte, naturally, was in the middle of eating a delicious piece of bean curd.

"The seafood chow mein is for you, Julie," Dad said. "Your favorite. We remember this."

"We could also try new things," Julie said. "We've only tried, like, one percent of the menu. Or we could go to another restaurant. There are lots of Chinese restaurants in Toronto."

"But why go somewhere else when we know this place is good?"

Charlotte remembered coming to Congee Princess back when she was in high school, when they'd go to Toronto for a day. Her parents were creatures of habit in some ways.

She looked around at her family and felt thankful she hadn't grown up in a situation like Mike's. Not that she'd say such mushy thoughts out loud. Her parents would probably think she had food poisoning or had secretly gotten a brain transplant.

She grabbed another piece of eggplant with her chopsticks and stuffed it in her mouth.

Eggplant. Heh.

"What are you smiling about, Charlotte?" Dad asked.

"I wasn't smiling," Charlotte protested.

"I bet she was thinking about her new boyfriend," Julie said.

All eyes were immediately on Charlotte.

She sent her sister a death glare. "Didn't you say you'd had your best month ever on your Etsy store?" She needed to deflect attention away from her.

"Yes." Julie beamed, though she was clearly bracing herself for what would come next.

"And I hear you got a new job?" Dad said. "At a cider bar?"

"The one where Charlotte drinks with her friends. Yep."

"It's time you got a real job. Like Charlotte."

Charlotte felt guilty for turning the attention to Julie's work, but she really hadn't wanted to talk about her boyfriend. Plus, their parents were going to talk about Julie's employment situation at some point anyway, though maybe it wouldn't have happened for another ten minutes if Charlotte hadn't mentioned her sister's Etsy store.

"Charlotte's boyfriend is Mike Guo," Julie said.

"Julie!" Charlotte hissed.

"Is this true?" Mom asked.

"Yes." Charlotte stabbed a piece of bean curd with her chopstick.

"Why do you sound angry? Is he not treating you right?" Dad's voice had an edge to it.

"No, he's treating me well."

"She just doesn't want to deal with all your questions," Julie said.

Yeah, and if you hadn't said anything, I wouldn't have to.

"You don't want us to ask questions?" Mom turned to Charlotte. "Wah, you know this isn't possible. We have so many. What's he doing now?"

"He's a financial planner at a bank."

"It's good to marry a financial planner. He will know what you should do with your money. Good for retirement."

Charlotte choked on her chow mein. "Thanks, Mom. That's exactly why I'm dating him."

"Unless he's bad at his job," Julie said. "Then you might lose all your money."

"I'm sure Mike is not a bad financial planner," Dad said. "He was a smart boy. This is a good career, don't you think, Julie? You should consider it."

Julie smacked her face with her hand.

And Charlotte, as annoyed as she was that Julie had mentioned Mike, understood her sister's frustration.

She and Julie didn't have much in common. They'd both enjoyed arts and crafts as kids, but that was about it. They were otherwise completely different in interests, skills, and temperament.

Charlotte couldn't imagine being a waitress or doing any

kind of job that involved customer service. That sounded like a nightmare. But Julie didn't seem to mind, and their parents were hung up on the fact that she'd never had a "prestigious" job.

Fortunately for Julie, the conversation quickly turned back to Mike.

"Is he handsome?" Mom asked. "I bet he's handsome now. Show me a picture."

"I don't have a picture," Charlotte said.

"There might be a picture of him on the bank's website. Or Facebook." Mom pulled out her phone.

"Fine, fine." Charlotte grabbed her own phone. "I'll show you his Facebook profile."

"Ugh. Facebook," Julie said. "You guys are so old."

"What's wrong with Facebook?" Mom frowned. "I thought it was cool and hip."

Charlotte and Julie looked at each other, similar expressions on their faces for once.

"I used it to find my university classmate," Mom said. "We hadn't seen each other in thirty years, and she's in Tokyo now... Oh, is that his picture? Handsome, yes. Nice smile. You should find a man like this, Julie."

Julie heaved out a sigh. "I won't date a financial planner."

"That's okay," Dad said. "We will settle for a doctor or pharmacist."

"*Settle* for a doctor. You're funny."

"Mike had such a crush on Charlotte when you were kids," Mom said.

"He told me," Charlotte said. "Apparently everyone knew but me."

"How could you not know? He followed you around like a lost puppy! And when you told him to shut up and draw in silence at the other end of the room, he listened."

"I did not tell him to *shut up*."

"Yes, you did. I scolded you for it." Mom reached for the scallops. "How are his parents?"

It was inevitable they'd come to this topic eventually, which was part of the reason Charlotte hadn't wanted to talk about Mike yet.

"He doesn't speak to them anymore," she said.

"What do you mean? Only once a month?"

"No. Not at all. His parents were terrible—did you know that? They were awful to him and his sister."

Mom and Dad looked at each other.

"Sometimes we wondered," Mom said, "but we didn't know anything for sure."

"You could have called the Children's Aid Society," Charlotte said. "Asked them to look into it."

"We weren't raised in this country. We didn't know much about these things, and whether they would treat families like his —or ours—fairly. Whether they would understand. And we heard bad stories about the foster system."

Charlotte couldn't help wondering what might have been different for Mike and Angela if there had been some kind of intervention. But what would talking about it do? It was the past.

"That's why we let him come over so much," Mom said. "We wouldn't have let you have friends over on school nights, but I thought maybe he was avoiding something at home and it was better for him to be with us when his parents let him. Plus, he didn't distract you much. You would do your homework together, and he was nice and polite. Why don't you invite him to meet up with us today? Where does he live?"

"No, I'm not ready for that."

"Okay. In two weeks, then." Mom poured everyone more tea.

"Two weeks?" Charlotte sputtered.

"You have a wedding next weekend, yes? The following weekend, you and Mike will come to Ashton Corners, what do you think?" She elbowed Dad, as if to say, *Isn't this clever?*

Charlotte sighed.

"You can even sleep in the same room," Mom said.

Charlotte choked on her shrimp. "What? You never let Brad—"

"But now you're over thirty."

"That's the age requirement to share a room with a man?" Julie asked.

"I don't know what you do in Toronto." Mom waved her hand away from her. "Don't tell me. But in my house, that is the rule."

"I thought the rule was not until we're engaged. You just made this up because you like Mike, and Charlotte is getting old."

"Hey!" Charlotte said.

"Well, I've been thinking," Mom said. "It's the twenty-first century. Maybe I should be flexible."

"It's been the twenty-first century for most of my life," Julie grumbled.

"So, you will bring Mike to visit us?" Mom asked Charlotte.

"I'll see what he thinks. He might have plans."

"I'm sure he's still like a puppy, eager to please you. Except with grown-up muscles."

"Maybe *I* don't want to go."

"But it would be so good to see you at home, and it's supposed to be a nice September. You can go to the beach and sunbathe. Even swim. The water will be much warmer than when you visited in June."

Reluctantly, Charlotte admitted it sounded a bit appealing. Especially the thought of seeing Mike in a bathing suit, though she could see him shirtless any night she wanted.

"You should come, too," Mom said to Julie.

"I have to work. And remember, I'm also working tonight, so if you want to go shopping, we should get going."

"Ah, you are right. You sure you don't want to come, Charlotte?"

"I'll pass, thank you."

"Might be for the best," Mom said. "You would just sulk in the corner the whole time."

"That's a bit of an exaggeration."

"Julie has better taste than you, and she's a better sport. She would not be sulking."

Julie stuck out her tongue at Charlotte, and Charlotte rolled her eyes.

Sometimes they still acted like they were kids.

"Though I know what size you are," Mom said. "Perhaps I will buy you something nice to wear on a date with Mike."

"Please don't." Charlotte shoved some bean curd in her mouth. "Last time you bought me a shirt, it had tassels on it."

"Why are you complaining? They were very stylish tassels. Weren't they, Julie?"

"It wasn't a completely terrible shirt, although I wouldn't have bought it for myself."

"You see?" Mom said to Charlotte. "Julie agrees it was just your style."

Charlotte shook her head. "That's not what she said. If you must buy me something today, how about another pair of pajama pants?"

"You're trying to mess with me." Mom shook her finger. "I know you don't need more pajamas. Or shirts with bad geology jokes."

Julie snorted.

"I can take care of my own clothes," Charlotte said. "Sometimes Nicole helps."

"Well, we will see if any cute tassels catch my eye."

"Mom!" Charlotte said, before realizing her mom was just trying to get a rise out of her.

Dammit, she hated when she fell for her family's bait.

Dad looked around the table. "Is everyone done eating? I'll ask them to pack up the food."

"I'm finished." Charlotte was stuffed.

"What are you doing for the bachelorette party tonight?" Mom asked. "I hope there will be lots of dancing. You always like dancing." She held her arms in the air and swayed.

"Very funny." Charlotte glanced around to see if anyone was looking at her mother. Fortunately not. She felt like a teenager embarrassed by her parents. "I'm not sure what we're doing. Sierra planned it."

Whatever they did, Charlotte hoped it would wipe the memory of this painful family lunch from her mind.

But no matter what, she would *not* be dancing.

[21]

THE DOORS OPENED, and Mike walked from the subway platform onto the train. He wasn't meeting Charlotte today—she had a bachelorette party—but he was going to have some late-afternoon drinks on a patio with Mason and Cody. Mason had been raving about the beer selection at this place.

Mike sat down on one of the red subway seats and was about to pull out his phone, maybe play a stupid game, when he noticed the older Asian man sitting across from him.

It looked like his father.

Mike clenched his hands into fists as his heart started beating uncomfortably fast.

Do you know how hard it is for me? To have a son who is such a disappointment?

He took another long look at the man, who was engrossed in a book and thankfully didn't notice him staring.

No, Mike didn't think that was his father.

But he hadn't seen his father in eight years, not since he'd told his parents that he wouldn't be speaking to them anymore. They'd hurled insults at him and tried to make him feel guilty for abandoning them.

Mike's gaze shifted to the right, landing on a woman of about sixty who looked nothing like his mother. She had a big sun visor perched on her head and was also reading a book.

Though it was possible his parents had gotten divorced and his father had remarried…

The man glanced up and caught Mike looking, and Mike offered him a small smile and nod, which the man returned before looking back at his book.

Definitely not his dad. Merely a doppelgänger.

Still, Mike couldn't help feeling unsettled, and those old feelings of guilt returned.

Good sons were not supposed to abandon their parents as they got older. They were supposed to take care of them. His parents were likely spinning sob stories about how their adult children refused to talk to them, gaining sympathy from people who didn't know the whole story. They would portray Mike as a monster and say they didn't know why they'd been cut out of their children's lives.

But this was what he and Angela needed. He did not owe anything to people who had treated him so horribly. He should not let himself feel guilty.

I am okay.

I did the right thing.

Sure, he wasn't one of those men with a crappy childhood who'd built an empire to prove everyone wrong. Mike's life was modest, but it was a good life. He had an apartment and a job that he was reasonably good at. He had friends. He even had a girlfriend, and she got rid of spiders for him and thought he was pretty great.

When he got off the subway in the east end, he was still slightly unsettled, even though he'd spent many minutes trying to give himself positive self-talk.

He was nearly at the bar when his phone vibrated. He took it out and smiled when he saw the text was from Charlotte.

My parents invited us to visit them in two weeks. We can stay overnight and they'll even, shockingly, let us share a room. They're very excited we're dating and want to see you again. I didn't mean to tell them yet, I promise, but Julie opened her big mouth.

Meeting his girlfriend's parents—yeah, they definitely weren't taking it slow. But he already knew these people. True, they hadn't seen him in twenty years, but still.

They *wanted* to see him.

When he was a child, these were the parents he'd wished for. He wanted to see them, too.

This would be easier than meeting a girlfriend's parents whom he'd never met before. In that case, he'd be really nervous, afraid they'd treat him like his own parents did.

You can say no, Charlotte texted. *It's soon, I know. And I'm not sure how fun it would be, though we could go to the beach, if the weather's nice.*

He was already thinking of Charlotte in a bathing suit.

Well, he wasn't sure Charlotte would wear the sort of bathing suit he had in mind, but he was sure she'd look great nonetheless.

Sure, I'd be happy to go, he replied.

He got to the bar and snagged the last table on the patio. Mason and Cody weren't here yet, so when he got another text message, he looked at it immediately.

It was from his sister.

You want to visit us on Labor Day weekend?

Sorry, I've got a wedding, he replied.

Who's getting married?

A friend of my girlfriend's.

YOU HAVE A GIRLFRIEND?

Quit yelling.

He wasn't surprised when his phone rang a minute later.

"I wasn't yelling," Angela said, by way of greeting. "It was a text message."

"Well, you're yelling now," he said.

"I'm just surprised, that's all. What about the weekend after Labor Day?"

"We're, uh, going to see her parents. You know Charlotte Tam, she lived next to us—"

"You're dating Charlotte?"

"Yeah, it's a long story. We met at a bar, and she asked me to teach her how to date—"

"She asked you to give her dating lessons? You?"

"Stop laughing. She thought I was some kind of dating expert because of my charm and good looks."

"Right."

"Anyway, at some point we decided to start dating for real." *After she proposed we have practice sex...* And because it was on his mind, and he wanted his sister to stop laughing, and she was the one person who'd understand, he said, "I saw Dad's doppelgänger on the subway today and it freaked the fuck out of me. All these ridiculous thoughts started running through my head. The words they used to say to us."

"You're too sensitive."

Angela didn't seem to be in the mood to empathize today.

"Sorry," she said a moment later.

He sighed. Any conversation about their parents put them both on edge. "It's okay. We'll see each other soon, alright? But the weekend after we go to Ashton Corners is Charlotte's birthday, so probably not then."

He ended the call, and a few minutes later, Mason and Cody slipped into the chairs across from him. A nice afternoon with his friends. Just what he needed to forget about his parents.

He wondered how Charlotte's bachelorette party was going. She'd be meeting her friends around now, too.

God, he'd been so shaken just from seeing a man who looked like his father. Had he really moved on from his past enough for a relationship?

~

"We're having a food crawl?" Charlotte asked Sierra.

They were sitting in the living room of Sierra and Amy's house, the one that Amy had inherited from her great aunt. Once she was married, she'd move to Victor's house, which was right next door. The plan was for Rose to live at the house with Sierra once Rose's lease was up—she'd recently talked to Sierra and Amy about it.

Amy was currently upstairs, getting ready.

"Yeah," Sierra said. "We'll go to lots of small plates and dessert places. There will be alcohol, too, don't worry. What's the problem? Amy will like it, and it's not like we're doing karaoke."

Charlotte bristled at the thought of karaoke. Saying karaoke was not her thing was an understatement.

"There's no problem," Charlotte said. "It's a good idea. It's just that I had lunch with my family, and I'm still full. Not sure how much I'll be able to eat."

Amy walked down the stairs, wearing a polka dot dress and a sash that said "Bride-to-be." She had a tiara perched on her head.

"Let's get this night started!" Amy said. "Where are we going first?"

They met everyone else at a place called Unicorn Bar. In addition to Charlotte, Sierra, Nicole, and Rose, there were a few of Amy's friends from the university where she was currently doing her master's degree.

Amy squealed in delight over her seven-layer rainbow cake—each layer was a different color. Charlotte didn't need any food, but she tried to get in the spirit by drinking something called a Glitter Bomb, which contained a truly appalling quantity of edible glitter.

Next, they went to an izakaya. Charlotte still wasn't hungry, but she couldn't help herself from eating takoyaki. She did love octopus balls.

Then they all crammed into a place that served Japanese soufflé pancakes. No alcohol here; instead, Charlotte got a coffee, and she helped herself to some of the tiramisu pancakes.

"Victor and I come here every few months," Amy said. "It was one of our first dates."

Charlotte couldn't help thinking about her own bachelorette party. They would not, of course, go to Unicorn Bar. Or do karaoke. And she would not wear a tiara or a goddamn sash. But it could be fun to do something other than hanging out at Ossington Cider Bar with her friends. Maybe they could go to Nautilus, which had been one of her first dates—well, practice dates—with Mike Guo.

"How are things going with Mike?" Amy asked.

"What?" Charlotte jumped and practically spilled her coffee— now that would have been a disaster. "We don't need to talk about my dating life. This is your bachelorette party. *Your* night."

"And I want to hear about Mike. As the bride-to-be, I demand you tell me."

Charlotte sighed. "It's going well. He cooked for me and brought me triple chocolate cake and flowers when I had menstrual cramps."

"Aw."

She didn't mention Mike's past, or how they both seemed to find it too good to be true.

Or how he'd caught her singing "Beauty and the Beast" in the shower.

"How are you feeling about getting married?" Charlotte asked.

"Oh, I'm so excited!" Amy said. "It's going to be a great day."

Even Charlotte found Amy's energy a little infectious today, and she smiled.

Sierra certainly did have a full night planned. They had tapas after the soufflé pancakes, and Charlotte ate too many olives and bacon-wrapped dates. This was followed by a place that special- ized in Indian street food.

But they still weren't done.

They went to an ice cream shop, where Amy got a black cone with coconut ice cream that was also black thanks to activated charcoal, and she asked for it to be covered in rainbow sprinkles.

Charlotte ordered the same thing. Without the sprinkles, of course.

She was sure it tasted good both ways.

By the time they rolled into Ossington Cider Bar, they were absolutely stuffed and rather drunk, and Amy had put her tiara on Nicole's head. Sierra, the weirdo that she was, still insisted on ordering her caramelized Brussels sprouts, but Charlotte stuck with a dry cider. Rose rested her head on Charlotte's shoulder.

"How are you doing today?" Charlotte asked quietly.

"Better, thanks. Just tipsy now. I'll find someone someday, won't I?"

"Of course." And Charlotte believed that. She was in an optimistic mood. If Rose wanted love, she was sure she'd find it.

It was nice to be out with her friends, celebrating with Amy, who'd be a married woman at this time next week.

Yet despite Charlotte's busy day, she was still looking forward to going out with Mike tomorrow, rather than spending all day at home in her pajamas.

"SHALL I get you another vanilla latte?" Mike asked, nodding at Charlotte's empty mug.

"Actually, I think I'll have a regular coffee now, thank you." She smiled at him. "Be quick so I can return to kicking your ass."

Mike suspected she'd do exactly that.

He chuckled as he got up from their cozy booth and went to the front of the boardgame café. It was called Checkers, and Charlotte had told him she'd wanted to go here for a while.

They'd started with Connect Four, mainly for nostalgic reasons. They'd played it quite a bit when they were kids. Specifically, the summer after grade three, they'd played it nearly every time he visited her. They'd kept a tally of all their games: she'd won a hundred and twenty-seven, and he'd won sixty-two.

He still remembered the exact numbers; he remembered a lot of things that had to do with Charlotte.

As adults, so far he'd won one game of Connect Four, and she'd won five.

They were now playing Innovation. One of the game experts at the café had explained the rules, then showed them the best

YouTube video to watch. At first, Mike had thought he and Charlotte were doing about equally, but now she kept repeating a particularly evil dogma that had nearly depleted his score pile, and she was one achievement away from winning.

Ah, well.

Charlotte had always been more competitive than he was.

He got his decaf latte and her coffee and headed back to their booth. He was feeling rather jittery today, so the last thing he needed was more caffeine, and he enjoyed the look of horror on Charlotte's face when he got something decaf.

"Here you go." He set her mug to her right, away from the cards. "One decaf coffee."

The look she gave him could probably kill little bunny rabbits.

Still, he thought her outraged expression was kind of cute.

"Of course it has caffeine," he said. "I don't have a death wish. Mine is decaf, however."

"Mike Guo, I'm disappointed in you." But her tone suggested she found him rather adorable, too.

He smiled before they resumed their game, but he continued to feel jittery and uneasy.

Back in the day, he'd always felt on edge, ready for the next disparaging comment or cruel action from his parents. That had simply been life, the inner turmoil he'd hidden with a smile.

But he wasn't accustomed to feeling like this anymore.

"Come on, pay up," Charlotte said. "Another card from your score pile."

He sighed and handed over the last card in his score pile. "You're gonna have to find something else to do now."

"You mean like winning?" When he didn't laugh, she leaned forward. "Is everything okay? Am I too competitive? I can tone it down."

He raised an eyebrow. "Oh, really."

"What is it?"

"I saw my father's doppelgänger in the subway yesterday." It sounded even more ridiculous now. "It reminded me of a whole bunch of shit. Like the time he said I could get a dog—this was after we moved to Etobicoke—and he took me to a shelter to pick one. I promised to do all the work, and I chose a dog named Wilbur."

"Like the pig in Charlotte's Web."

"Yeah, that's what I immediately thought of, too. I was all excited about bringing this dog home, and then my dad laughed and said it had all been a joke, did I seriously think he would ever let me get a dog?"

"Mike! What a shitty thing to do."

Charlotte came to sit on his side of the booth as it all flooded back to him. That story and so many others. But her hand on his shoulder…it did help.

"Would you want a dog now?" she asked.

"Maybe," he said. "Though I'm gone all day for work—"

"You know who's home all day, though? Me."

"Are you suggesting we move in together?"

She looked a little startled. "Right. We shouldn't move in together now, of course, but it's a possibility for the future. I'd like to have a dog, too." She returned to her side of the booth and picked up her cards. "My turn, isn't it?"

"Yeah." He swallowed. "Your turn."

It was a very, very hot August afternoon. By the time they got back to Charlotte's place, they were both sweating profusely after the short walk from the subway station.

It didn't surprise Mike that Charlotte had won their first game of Innovation, but he'd managed to sneak out a surprise victory in their second game.

They were arguing about strategy when they stepped into her apartment. It was slightly cooler than outside, but not much; however, she immediately turned on the air conditioner and a large fan, and it wasn't too bad.

"I got something for you," she said. "Sit at the table and I'll bring it to you."

A minute later, she set a cold bottle in front of him. He looked at the label, expecting beer or cider, but it was something else. "Root beer?"

"Why not?" she said. "You like root beer. Or, at least, you used to."

"I haven't had root beer in a long time."

"Well, I hope this is good. It's some kind of artisanal root beer. It probably still tastes like toothpaste, though." Charlotte had never liked root beer.

"You know what I haven't had in a *really* long time?" he said. "A root beer float."

"I expected this, you know."

She returned a moment later with a box of Chapman's vanilla ice cream, as well as two pint glasses.

She'd said "I love you" when he let her have the rest of the coffee the other day, but now he was tempted to say the same words to her. Just because she'd gotten him root beer and vanilla ice cream on a hot summer's day. He wasn't used to people doing thoughtful things for him.

Because I don't deserve it.

He squashed that thought. There was no reason he didn't deserve a root beer float right now. He didn't need to be a paragon of virtue to deserve such a thing, and he definitely didn't deserve to be treated like crap.

Yeah, he was going to enjoy the shit out of this float.

He grabbed Charlotte's hand and kissed her on the lips. He would have kissed her for hours, but the ice cream would melt.

Later. He'd kiss her more later.

"You got two glasses." He gestured toward them. "Are you having a root beer float, too?"

"Don't be ridiculous. I got the good stuff for me."

She returned to the kitchen and came back with a small bottle of Dr. Pepper, an ice cream scoop, and two long spoons.

"That's the good stuff?" He took a quick look at the label on his root beer. "Is that handcrafted with natural spring water? Does it have a sepia-toned photo of an old white dude with a beard? Nah, I didn't think so."

She didn't deign to reply, but her lips twitched.

"Alright, alright," he said. "Come here and have your sub-standard float with me."

This time, she rolled her eyes as she sat down.

She added a generous scoop of ice cream to each of their glasses, then slowly poured Dr. Pepper into hers as he poured root beer into his.

So foamy and delicious. The perfect treat for a hot day.

It reminded him of going next door to Charlotte's house in the summer. Occasionally, her mother would let them have freezies or ice cream. Sometimes floats.

He couldn't stop grinning.

As Charlotte stood at the front of the church, her childhood dream seemed closer than ever before.

Amy and Victor hadn't cared where their wedding was held, but their parents had wanted them to get married in a church, so here they were.

Charlotte had walked down the aisle a minute ago, in a blue dress and the tiniest of heels. Amy was making her entrance now, on her father's arm, and Charlotte was happy for her friend, who'd somehow managed to move to Toronto, find love, and get married, all in just over a year.

At the last wedding Charlotte had attended, she'd been rather sad, feeling like it was an impossible dream for her.

It didn't feel that way now.

She could imagine herself walking down the aisle in a wedding dress. Just as she'd imagined when she was a child.

She'd always found it weird that she wanted a wedding, given she didn't particularly like being the center of attention. But she'd have a small wedding, and no dances that everyone watched— God, no. No vows that she'd written herself.

But she'd have Mike.

Yes, the groom was clear in her mind now. It would be him.

She glanced at Mike, sitting in one of the pews near the back, and smiled.

After the ceremony, she met up with him outside the church. He was wearing a gray suit today and a pale pink tie, and he looked impossibly handsome. She couldn't help tilting her head up to kiss him.

"Your lipstick," he murmured.

"Whatever. I'll fix it later."

It was just a quick kiss on the lips, but she was still amazed by how much a quick kiss with him could make her feel.

"You've turned me into such a sap," she muttered.

"*I've* turned you into a sap? I think—"

"Don't tell me it could possibly be the other way. This is me, after all."

"You got me handcrafted root beer made with natural spring water."

"Oh, right. How could I forget, the fucking natural spring water and the old dude on the label? How romantic."

"I found it romantic," he said quietly.

The fabric of her dress felt even more uncomfortable now.

"I can't wait to get out of this dress," she said. "Purely for non-sexual reasons, of course."

He laughed as he caught her hand in his. "Sure, sure."

"Alright, you lovebirds," Sierra said. "Time for pictures."

Amy and Victor's close family, as well as the wedding party, were going to Edwards Gardens for pictures. Mike came with them, since he had nothing else to do, and after the pictures with the bridesmaids were finished, they walked around the gardens together.

He'd probably be alarmed if he knew she was thinking about *their* wedding.

Dinner was at a Chinese banquet hall in North York, and fortunately, there was no head table for the bridal party. Amy and Victor sat at a table with their parents, and Charlotte sat with her other friends, Mike by her side.

It was the first time he'd properly met her friends, and while she likely would have done a piss-poor job if their roles were reversed, he seemed at ease.

"Tell us what Charlotte was like as a child," Nicole said.

"Oh, she was very sweet and made flower crowns out of dandelions," Mike said with a smile.

Nicole snorted.

"Nah," he said, "though she did do some intricate drawings of butterflies. We used to draw a lot together. And play boardgames, which she usually won."

Mike teased Charlotte with such fondness, stroking her bare arm as he did so.

And sometime between the first two courses—roast suckling pig and deep-fried crab claws—he tilted his head to look at her... and she felt an embarrassing *whoosh* in her stomach and realized she loved him.

Those feelings only intensified with the scallops, then the bird's nest soup. She was pretty sure the aphrodisiac properties of bird's nest were bullshit, but still.

She'd only been in love once before, and in retrospect, it had been foolish of her to love Brad when he'd never understood and fully accepted who she was. Everything she'd felt for him had disappeared when he'd made her worst nightmare come true.

But this time, she knew it was different. Knew Mike wouldn't do something stupid that would make it all go away. Knew he cared for the person she truly was, and she cared for him in the same way.

The multi-course Chinese banquet took a long time, and it was late by the time the dancing started. Amy and Victor had their first dance together, and as soon as that was over, "Wannabe" started playing. Charlotte rolled her eyes at the Spice Girls song, which she was sure Amy had asked the DJ to play.

Her friends jumped up to dance with the bride, and Mike danced with them, too. Jumping around and moving his hips and making her laugh. He held out his hands and beckoned her toward him, but when she shook her head and stayed seated, he didn't try to drag her up.

Watching him dance was better than actually dancing.

A little later, there was a slow song, and he came back to her and held out a hand, and she was so full of love that she actually stood up to dance. She didn't recognize the song, but she was barely aware of it anyway. He didn't try any fancy moves, just put his hands on her waist as she put hers around his neck and they swayed together.

"You good?" he murmured, pushing back a lock of hair that had escaped her updo.

"Yes, except my feet are killing me. I'm not used to wearing shoes like this. I know the heel is small, but—"

He wrapped his arms securely around her and lifted her up so her toes were an inch off the ground. She laughed.

"Better?" he asked.

She nearly said it to him, and not about coffee this time. *I love you.*

But it was too soon, wasn't it? She'd keep it to herself.

For now.

~

Mike had been to many weddings over the years, but never with a date.

Today, he was at a wedding of people he'd never met before, but he'd come with Charlotte, and it was great. And overwhelming.

He kept thinking about their wedding.

At first, it was the little details. Like, would they have bird's nest soup?

They wouldn't have shark's fin soup, of course—that practice was horrible. Bird's nest soup was a common alternative, but it was expensive, and it didn't seem like good financial sense to spend lots of money on a soup made of hardened bird saliva, especially when he'd never been overly impressed by it. There were probably issues with harvesting those nests, too.

He'd asked Charlotte what she thought of bird's nest soup, and she shrugged and said it was okay, and he filed that away in his mental cabinet of everything he knew about her.

He also found himself wondering if she'd want a first dance together. Probably not.

That was fine.

On one hand, thinking of marrying Charlotte was the easiest thing in the world.

On the other hand…

How could he do this?

Victor had lots of family here, but Mike wouldn't have much family. Just his sister and Bailey, and maybe his aunt, uncle, and two cousins.

Shame washed over him. There would be only one set of parents at the wedding, but it wasn't his fault. It was his parents' fault for being terrible people, and he had no intention of being part of their lives again.

For one, he would never want to subject Charlotte to them.

This woman, whom he'd wanted when he was a gangly boy… as he held her in his arms, he couldn't help thinking she was too good for him, as he'd thought all those years ago.

In some ways, it was damn hard to imagine marrying her.

Because it seemed too amazing to be true.

[23]

SINCE NEITHER OF them owned a car, they'd rented one for the weekend. Charlotte wanted to drive, and Mike was happy to let her do so.

In a way, it was odd being in a car with her in the driver's seat. Another reminder of how grown up they were. When he'd left Ashton Corners, he'd still been a few years away from being old enough to drive, and now, he was going back for the first time since he'd left. Since that horrible morning when his parents had woken him up and given him one hour to pack.

He was looking forward to seeing the beach, the playground.

Most of all, to seeing Charlotte's parents.

The rural scenery started to feel familiar as they approached the "Welcome to Ashton Corners" sign. It was a different sign from before, and the population had shrunk by fifty people.

The Tim Hortons had also been renovated. The elementary school looked the same as before, although there were no longer two portables at the back.

As they drove along Main Street, Mike started to feel nervous, which he hadn't expected.

When Charlotte parked in her parents' driveway, he got out

of the car and regarded the house next door. The porch had been redone and—

"Mike!" Mrs. Tam cried, hurrying down the driveway. She'd forgotten to put on her shoes and was still wearing pink slippers. "So good to see you again. You are very handsome. I knew you would be."

"Mom," Charlotte said, opening the trunk.

Mike rushed to grab the suitcases so she wouldn't do it all herself.

"Is this your car?" Mrs. Tam asked.

"No, I don't have a car. We rented it for the weekend." He braced himself, somehow expecting her to be disappointed.

But she said, "This is best, if you don't need one in the city. Just rent a car a few times a year when you need it and save more money for your RRSP. Smart, yes? Charlotte says you're a financial planner."

"That's right, Mrs. Tam."

"You should call me Bonnie. Ah, you're carrying both suitcases. Good that you have nice muscles."

"Those suitcases are only five pounds each," Charlotte said. "We're just here for one night." She'd decided it would be better to drive up Saturday morning rather than going on Friday, and since it was a fairly hot September weekend, it wasn't like the clothes were heavy.

Mrs. Tam—Bonnie—was now peering closely at his hair.

"What on earth are you doing?" Charlotte asked.

"Checking to see if his hairline is receding," Bonnie said, as though this were an ordinary thing to do. "No, he has very thick hair."

"Thanks to my special shampoo," he said, and she laughed.

He and Charlotte followed her inside.

"I made your favorite for lunch," Bonnie said. "I assume you still like lor mai fun. But if not, it's okay, I can make something else."

"No, no, it sounds wonderful," he assured her. He loved her sticky rice with Chinese sausage, dried mushrooms, and dried shrimp, and the stuff he'd had at restaurants hadn't been as good as hers.

They took off their shoes, left the suitcases in the front hall, and headed to the kitchen. When Charlotte squeezed his hand, he almost snatched it away, feeling like they were doing something illicit.

But her parents knew of their relationship and were happy about it. Hand-holding was pretty tame.

"Hi, Mr. Tam," he said to the man who was setting the table. He couldn't remember Charlotte's father's first name.

"Albert." He shook Mike's hand.

The Tams had gotten a new table, which wasn't surprising since it had been twenty years, but otherwise, the kitchen felt very similar. A rice cooker sat on the counter. There was a pot of tea in the center of the table.

It was a little like coming home.

They sat down for lunch—the aforementioned sticky rice, plus snow peas stir-fried with shrimp—and it was delicious, as he told Bonnie more than once. She insisted on giving him seconds of everything, saying he would need lots of energy for...

Charlotte cut her mother off with another outraged "Mom!"

They'd probably be talking in Cantonese if it wasn't for him, but Mike didn't speak Cantonese, other than the few words he'd learned from Charlotte. His Mandarin was pretty poor, too. For him, Mandarin was the language he used for speaking to his parents, and his skills had deteriorated since he'd cut contact with them. He should have tried to practice, but it was tangled up with complicated feelings.

Charlotte's parents didn't say anything about wishing he were a surgeon who spoke Cantonese. Nope, they seemed happy with him just the way he was.

And Charlotte kept her hand on his thigh during lunch, and

when they went up to her old bedroom to put away their suit-cases, he pinned her against the wall and kissed her.

"Mike!" she said. "Don't you want to go to the beach and see me in a bikini?"

That got his attention. "We're going to the beach now? And you're wearing a bikini?"

"Yeah, you're lucky I like you so much. You remembered to bring your swimsuit, didn't you? Tiny little Speedo?"

He laughed. "Not so much."

Though he was excited to go to the beach, he spent a moment looking around the room before opening his suitcase. The furni-ture was all in the same place as before, but there was little else in the room. A lot of stuff had been cleared out.

There was, however, a small binder on the desk labeled "Charlotte's Drawings, Ages 2-12." He opened it up.

The first few were scribbles in crayon. Her parents had place them in sheet protectors and lovingly labeled each one.

A bunny pooping. Charlotte, age 2.

Mommy cooking dinner. Charlotte, age 2.

Frosty the Snowman. Charlotte, age 3.

Baby Julie crying because she wants milk. Charlotte, age 3.

The playground. Charlotte, age 3.

A polar bear playing with a seal. Charlotte, age 4.

A cow's udder. Charlotte, age 4.

Then there was a letter, written by someone who was decid-edly older than three or four.

Dear Mr. Garbageman, My mom threw out my drawings. It was an accident and she is very sorry. If you find them, can you please return them?

He laughed. "What's this?"

Charlotte looked over his shoulder. "My mom didn't think it was necessary to keep all seventeen drawings I drew each day. She doubted I'd notice, but I did, so I made her write a letter to the garbageman. Which she obviously didn't send."

Mike kept flipping through the binder, a bit overwhelmed by the care her parents had taken to put this together. His parents would never have done anything like this, but one day, he'd keep his own children's artwork.

And then he saw something that made him stare for a full minute.

He didn't remember this drawing, but apparently, he was the one who'd done it.

Charlotte. The letters were written in blue pencil crayon, a mix of capitals and lowercase, and at the bottom of the page, her mom or dad had written: *A portrait of Charlotte by Mike Guo, age 6. She is wearing a purple shirt because purple is her favorite color, and she is frowning because she doesn't like having her picture taken.*

"Your parents kept a picture that I drew?" he asked, his throat clogged with emotion.

"Well, you drew a picture of me, so it was important."

Yes, but still. "I bet it's the only drawing from my childhood that exists."

"Nope. Turn the page."

He did, and he found himself staring at a picture of John Olerud that he'd drawn for her, twenty-five years ago.

"Probably worth a fortune now," Charlotte said.

"Just like all those eggplants you drew at the bar."

She snorted before giving him a kiss. He walked backward and toppled onto the bed with her, wincing when his head hit the wall on the other side.

It was only a twin bed. Not a queen, like they both had in their apartments.

"So, we're supposed to share this bed?" he asked.

"We don't have to. One of us can sleep in Julie's room. But outside of my parents' room, there are only twin beds in the house. And since my parents like you so much, they aren't going to force us to sleep separately."

He'd kept expecting something to go wrong today, but so far, everything was going right.

But there was still lots of time for it all to go to shit.

~

It was a ten-minute walk to the beach. Charlotte was wearing shorts and a non-geology-related T-shirt over her bathing suit, an ugly sunhat on her head. She'd planned to wear her Blue Jays cap, but her mom had protested that it didn't cover her ears and the back of her neck, and had instead given her this oversized straw sunhat with a pink ribbon tied around the middle.

It was truly ridiculous, but Mike had said she looked cute, so she hadn't put up too much of a fuss when her mother pushed her out the door in it.

He was wearing green swim trunks that went practically to his knees, a white T-shirt, and her Blue Jays hat. He carried their bag of towels, books, water, and sunscreen.

"I thought you didn't like the beach?" he said. "Or has that changed?"

"I still hate swimming." Stepping into cold water was like having to wear pants with a zipper and a button—something she avoided if possible. "But I thought it might be fun to lie on the beach with you."

"You mean you want to see me half-naked."

Though they weren't at the beach yet, he pulled the T-shirt over his head and stuffed it into the bag, then did a macho strut that made her laugh.

He seemed to be having a good time, for the most part, but she'd sensed today was a little hard for him. Seeing his old house, her parents, their childhood artwork.

For someone who didn't talk to his parents and had never met a girlfriend's parents before, eating lunch with hers and having them fawn all over him... Well, that would probably stir up feelings.

There were moments when she could tell he was swallowing hard or recalling an unhappy memory, but she didn't think they were obvious to anyone else. They were only obvious to her because she was so in touch with him now, like their hearts were beating as one or some such nonsense.

There was only a small section of usable beach in Ashton Corners, and so the town had never really built up a tourism industry. It was mainly locals who went to the beach, similar to Mosquito Bay farther south. If you wanted a bigger, busier beach, you went to Grand Bend.

They claimed a spot at the edge of the beach, not too close to anyone else. She pulled off her shorts and T-shirt and was about to apply sunscreen when he said, "We're going in the water first."

"I'm not getting wet. Yes, it's late summer, but it's Lake Huron."

"Fortunately, you're not going to get wet."

He crouched down, and it took her a moment to realize what he wanted her to do. She hopped on his back, her arms around his neck, and he hurried into the water. She couldn't help laughing. She'd taken off her sunhat, and her hair blew behind her in the breeze. Although droplets of water hit her lower legs, she wasn't getting very wet, not when she was clinging to Mike.

"You better not drop me in the lake," she said.

"Don't worry, I would never."

Since he wasn't the sort of asshole who'd immediately break his word, he waded out a little deeper, until her toes were grazing the water, then made his way back to shore.

When he set her down, he turned her so she was facing him. He stepped into her personal space, but she didn't mind, even though they were in public. In fact, she gripped his solid arms as he kissed her.

"Alright, let's get started on the sunscreen," he said, gesturing for her to lie down.

She pulled her hair into a ponytail, then lay on her stomach, arms crossed under her head.

He started with her legs. She could have done her legs herself, as well as her arms, but she wasn't complaining. There was something about the slow, deliberate way he was applying the sunscreen that made goose bumps break out on her skin, even in the hot sun.

Next, he used his large hands to run the sunscreen into her back, and she felt like she was melting into her towel.

"I wish this beach was private," she murmured.

"Do you, now? What would you like to do? Tell me in explicit detail."

She reached back to slap him at his teasing tone.

"You want me to put sunscreen on you now?" she asked.

"Nah, I'm going swimming first."

Charlotte had meant to read her book, but this piqued her attention. She turned so she was looking toward the water and propped her chin in her hands. "I'm waiting for the show."

Mike jogged to the lake and waded out to his waist. Although he was far away, she still enjoyed looking at him. He waved at her, and she felt a strange sense of pride that she was his.

He dove under the surface, emerging a few seconds later and doing a short stretch of the front crawl before diving under again. When he walked back onto the beach, his skin was glistening with water, and she stupidly wanted to lick it.

He sat down and she started applying sunscreen to his broad shoulders, but it turned into a massage.

"You're tense," she said. Though he'd been acting easy with her for the last hour, she wasn't surprised.

She wished she could be closer to him. Take him inside her, touch his skin in a way that would tell him he was okay—better than okay.

"Charlotte," he groaned. "You'll have to stop that if you want me to survive the day."

She moved in front of him, and though she didn't think she'd ever done something that could be called a "shimmy" in her life, she did so now, hoping to draw attention to her boobs.

Even if her shimmy was hardly high quality, it worked; he had what could only be described as bedroom eyes.

"If you keep that up, I'm going to flex," he said warningly.

"Aw, what a threat."

But it was.

She was a freaking sweaty, goose-bumpy, turned-on mess. She wasn't sure she'd survive this, either.

And then he sat up and flexed his left arm.

She rolled her eyes and pretended to be unimpressed. "You're such a show-off."

"Just around you."

"Yeah, I know you like picking on me, but I'm not impressed by your flexing, shirtless, pineapple-on-pizza-loving ways."

His burst of laughter made the couple nearby look at them.

"Yeah, you are, Charlotte."

Yes, she was.

But it was still many, many hours before she got to be naked with him.

[24]

WHEN CHARLOTTE and Mike returned to the house, her parents had not, unfortunately, taken up golf or croquet or a similar hobby that would get them outdoors. Instead, they insisted on—horror upon horrors—looking at old photo albums with Mike. As he'd noted when drawing his portrait of six-year-old Charlotte, she hated having her picture taken, and she was scowling in nearly every picture from her childhood.

Although there was one of her and Mike, sitting on the front steps, in which she didn't look completely miserable.

By the time they'd eaten dinner, played mahjong with her parents, and gotten ready for bed, it was eleven o'clock. As soon as Charlotte returned from the washroom, Mike scooped her up and placed her on the bed.

"So, we're doing this?" he whispered, covering her body with his. "In your parents' house? I'm willing to wait until we get back to Toronto, if you'd prefer…" His lips twitched.

She kissed him to put an end to any other silly things he was going to say, and he kissed her back just as eagerly. He shifted against her, his cock hardening.

There was something perversely thrilling about doing this on her childhood bed, after her parents had gone to sleep, even if she was thirty-two years old. She'd never had sex on this bed before, but she didn't tell Mike that.

She just pulled his T-shirt over his head.

She'd seen him without a shirt earlier, but now, she slid her hands over his abs and pecs and around to his back, reveling in each inch of him she got to touch.

When she started bucking against him, he gave her a lopsided grin and rolled off her before removing each flimsy piece of clothing she was wearing. Sometimes he practically tore her clothes off, but not tonight. They'd been waiting all day to be together like this, but he removed each one slowly, kissing her skin as it was revealed to him.

Once she was naked, he slipped his hand between her legs and parted her folds. She whimpered as he slid his finger inside her, rolling his thumb over her clit at the same time.

But her parents were just in the other room. She had to be quiet.

She pulled down his shorts and boxers and wrapped her hand around his erection. She saw heat flare in his eyes, but he made no sound as they stroked each other.

And when she knelt beside him and took his cock in her mouth, he made no noise then, either, but she was an expert on reading his body now, and she could tell how he felt.

Oh, who was she kidding. She was giving him a blowjob. He was obviously enjoying himself. But she could see it in every move and look he made, too.

When she took him particularly deep in her mouth, she heard his sharp intake of breath, saw the way he was gripping the sheets, and God, she wanted him.

She hopped off the bed and grabbed a condom and lube. He prepared himself, and she couldn't help squirming. He positioned his cock at her entrance, and when he slid inside, she had to cover her mouth because it felt so amazing and she wanted to make noise.

He bent down to kiss her, and she savored his taste, his soapy scent.

He pulled out and thrust back inside her.

Screech.

That wasn't her; her gasp had been muffled by the sound of the bed.

He thrust inside her again.

Screech.

He silently shook with laughter, as did she.

This was what she got for never having sex in her childhood bed before; she hadn't known it would be so damn loud. The screeches pierced the silence of the night in Ashton Corners.

He pulled out of her and tugged her out of bed, maneuvering her in front of the desk. He bent her over it and slid into her from behind.

"Okay?" he murmured in her ear, the first time either of them had spoken in a long time.

She nodded.

He pumped into her, and her fingers gripped the edge of the desk. Her breasts were pressed against the surface. She just felt so *much,* and it was all part of being with Mike.

She pushed her ass back against him and he growled—quietly, of course. He leaned down and swept her hair to the side before pressing kisses up and down her neck, her jaw, her shoulder. His hand slipped between her legs again and rubbed her clit, and it didn't take much before she was gripping the desk even more tightly and shuddering against the surface. He sped up his pace and came a moment later.

After cleaning up, they put on their pajamas and returned to bed. It screeched a bit as Mike got on, and they both smiled. He turned Charlotte onto her side and held her from behind—it would be impossible to sleep any other way on the small bed.

She wanted to break the silence.

I love you, she wanted to say.

But she could tell he wasn't ready to hear it.

Instead, she said, "Sleep well."

Even though they'd had a fun day together, even though he'd laughed and teased her and carried her into the lake, she had her doubts that his mind would let him sleep.

It was painful to know someone so well, but although he was turning her insides to mush, she wouldn't have it any other way.

It was three in the morning, and Mike still hadn't slept.

Hello, insomnia, my old friend.

Back in the days when he'd lived with his parents, he'd often had trouble sleeping. When they'd found him wandering the house in the middle of the night, they'd say he wasn't working hard enough and that was why he wasn't tired and couldn't fall asleep.

But insomnia didn't mean you weren't tired; you could be exhausted and unable to sleep.

He extricated himself from Charlotte's limbs and sat at her old desk. He flipped on the small lamp, looking over to make sure it didn't wake her, and studied her childhood drawings again.

And *his* childhood drawing of her. Scowling because she didn't like pictures. Ha.

Charlotte had always been so sure of who she was, and she hadn't tried to change it, hadn't made apologies for it.

Mike, on the other hand...well, whoever he was, it wasn't enough for his parents, and so he'd wanted to be someone else.

Charlotte was smart and talented, and he'd known, when he developed a massive crush on her all those years ago, that she could do much better than him.

Quietly, he got up from the desk. He opened the window, the side where there was no screen, and stuck his head out.

After two decades of living in Toronto, it was almost eerily quiet.

And if he stuck his head out farther, he could see what had been his bedroom window.

He glanced back at Charlotte's desk. Along with the old drawings, there was a box of Laurentien pencil crayons, which she'd gotten for Christmas one year. It was the only thing she'd wanted for Christmas. Sixty colors—it had seemed magical when they were little. She'd let him use them, of course.

His parents had never bought him a gift that he'd wanted, not even a small one. Sometimes they'd buy big gifts that they knew he'd hate, then make him feel ungrateful.

God, he was so messed up.

He was a fucked-up ordinary guy, and Charlotte...she was extraordinary.

He carefully shut the window, turned off the lamp, then climbed into bed. She made a soft sound in her sleep as she rolled over.

She's too good for you.

He'd spent years working on getting those stupid thoughts out of his head.

He was a decent person, and he'd never treat anyone the way his parents had treated him and Angela. Their actions had nothing to do with his value as a person. Plus, Charlotte brought out the best in him and showed that she liked him in every little thing she did.

Mike *knew* this.

But.

Romantic relationships had scared him for years. Even after he'd started feeling better about himself, the idea of that kind of intimacy had made him uneasy.

With Charlotte, it was simple, yet at the same time, it wasn't.

Looking at the house next door—it had given him a full-body shudder. Yep, Ashton Corners made him feel like more of a mess than he'd been in years.

Today had been such a fucking roller coaster. Memories tied up in so many things, like a box of pencil crayons.

New memories, too. Like bending Charlotte over her childhood desk.

Seeing her in a bikini.

Playing mahjong with her parents like he belonged there. They were excited that he was with Charlotte, but he still had trouble truly believing it.

He carefully, so carefully, wrapped his arm around her, and she made a sound of contentment. Like even in her sleep, she enjoyed being next to him.

But would she always?

You don't deserve this. What are you thinking? You'll screw it up. You have no experience with these things.

He hadn't heard his father's voice in real life in eight years, but he could still hear it, clear as day, in his head.

As he finally, finally fell asleep, doubts still crowded his brain.

Could he really do this?

[25]

MIKE DIDN'T SLEEP for long. By seven, he was awake again, even though he usually had no trouble sleeping in on weekends.

When he sat up, Charlotte stirred, but she didn't wake up.

The morning light poured in through the vertical blinds, illuminating her face, and she looked so lovely that his breath caught in his throat.

He wanted to wake up with her every morning.

He loved her.

Not the way he'd loved her as a thirteen-year-old boy who'd barely begun his growth spurt, but as an adult, who knew so much more of the world. He'd met many other women, and even if he hadn't dated much, he knew she was the one he wanted.

The selfless thing would be to let her find someone better. Someone who knew about love, who hadn't grown up without it, then avoided it.

But the thought of walking away from her caused everything inside him to ache.

He put on some clothes and headed downstairs, needing to get out of the room.

"Ah, Mike! Good morning," Bonnie said.

"Good morning. Bonnie."

"Would you like coffee?" She gestured to the coffeepot.

Mike couldn't help smiling. Coffee, such an everyday thing, made him think of Charlotte now. When they were children, he hadn't known she'd grow up to be a coffee addict.

His throat suddenly felt dry and scratchy.

"Yes, coffee would be great," he said.

She poured him a mug and took out the milk and sugar; he added some to his cup.

"How's Angela doing?" she asked.

It was interesting that the first person she asked about was Angela. Had Charlotte told her that he didn't talk to his parents?

Well, he was glad he didn't need to have that conversation.

"She lives in Ottawa," he said. "She has a daughter named Bailey."

Bonnie smiled. "How old is Bailey? Is she in school yet?"

"She's ten, actually."

"So big! You and Charlotte will need to hurry up if you want children. Maybe you don't." She frowned. "I know she doesn't need to be a mother, but I will not lie, I will make a wonderful grandmother."

He chuckled. "One day, maybe. We'll see."

"What does Bailey like? What are her favorite subjects in school?"

"She, uh, likes poisonous frogs and mushrooms. She draws pictures of them."

"Like Charlotte, she is a weird kid." This was said with affection. "Perhaps she will be a biologist."

He chuckled again, at how Bonnie turned everything into a potential career.

Mike didn't mind talking to her, but he was still a bit on edge.

I love Charlotte.

He downed the rest of his coffee and stood up. "I'm going for a walk. Nice to get some fresh air in the morning, you know? Tell Charlotte where I am if she wakes up."

"Of course, of course." Bonnie paused. "Charlotte is very independent, and she can look after herself in her own strange way. She doesn't like to take nonsense from people, but she did this with her ex. You will be different, yes? I know you're a good boy, but I'm watching you." She pointed at him in the least threatening way possible.

When Mike got outside, he stood on the sidewalk in front of his old house, and all sorts of terrible memories came back to him. Like the time his parents had locked him outside, in freezing cold weather because his grades weren't good enough…

He started running, as though if he ran fast enough, it would all go away.

This town wasn't his home anymore, but he still knew the streets. He ran past the elementary school. The grocery store—a different name now, but it looked the same otherwise. The pharmacy. The convenience store that still had the same "Convenience & Video" sign, though it probably hadn't rented videos in years.

He stopped when he got to the park at the edge of town. It had been his favorite place because there was a weeping willow, and when he was behind the long branches that nearly touched the ground, he could pretend it was a secret hiding place where no one could see him.

He looked at his phone, glad to see he had a signal, and called Mason.

"Hey Mike, what's up?" Mason's voice was laced with concern.

Yeah, eight in the morning on a Sunday was a weird time for a phone call.

"You know how I was going to see Charlotte's family this weekend?" Mike said.

"Did the whole meet-the-parents thing not go well?"

"The parents are fine, but being back in Ashton Corners,

seeing the house where we lived…I'm freaking out. And I realized I love her, and God, I'm going to fuck this up, aren't I? I don't want to fuck it up, though. That's why I'm calling you."

As soon as Mike said all that, he regretted it. He and Mason didn't talk about this stuff.

But before he could tell Mason to forget it, his friend started speaking.

"If you have a long relationship with anyone," Mason said, "you're bound to fuck up a little. That's okay, and it doesn't mean you don't deserve love. You'll make things right. I've known you for many years, and I have no doubt you're good at romantic relationships, even if you don't have much experience. If I thought you were the kind of guy my sister would like, I would have set you up."

"Why wouldn't your sister like me?" Mike couldn't help bracing himself.

"Because you're not Goth enough."

Mike laughed. "Okay, that's fair."

"We're all a bit of a mess," Mason said, "and yes, I know what you have to deal with is different from what I do. But instead of setting fire to everything, you're doing the sensible, mature thing and calling me at eight-o-fucking-clock on a Sunday morning instead."

"Sorry."

"Don't be."

"Maybe I'm not ready for a relationship. I knew I wasn't before, but I thought—"

"I think you are, but it's complicated with this woman because she's part of your past, and you have to confront it in different ways than before. So, I think it's just a blip."

Mike ran a hand through his hair. "Right. Thanks, man."

"And what about her? She's good to you?"

"Yeah."

Mike had lacked examples of healthy relationships early in his life, but unlike his parents, Charlotte never seemed disappointed in who he was as a person, never yelled at him for being a failure. She appreciated him, but at the same time, she didn't consider him responsible for all her emotions. It seemed healthy to him.

He talked to Mason for a few more minutes, and then he called his sister.

"Hey," Angela said. "I'm making pancakes for breakfast. You jealous?"

Yep, that made his stomach rumble. "So jealous."

"Aren't you with Charlotte in Ashton Corners this weekend?" Angela made smooching noises, and in the distance, Mike thought he heard Bailey say, *Mom, please don't.*

"Yes. I love her, but—"

"I know where this is going. Mom and Dad? They were wrong about us. Don't let them *win*. They don't deserve it. Four years ago, I let them win. I went on several dates with a great guy, and then I blew it all up."

"You never told me—"

"I don't tell you everything, of course. And that's all I'm saying about it. Just don't be a fucking idiot."

"You gonna put money in the swear jar now?"

"Shut up."

"Thank you for always being a pain in my ass."

"Swear jar, Uncle Mike."

He put down his phone and settled against the trunk of the tree. Twenty years had passed since he was last here, but this tree had barely changed.

He'd changed, though.

~

There was nobody else in her bed.

Charlotte sat up and looked around the room. She often liked being alone, but Mike was supposed to be with her. She'd wanted to wake up with him.

She threw on some clothes and went downstairs, the smell of coffee beckoning. Mike was probably down here, charming her mother over breakfast.

But there was no one in the kitchen, just half a pot of coffee.

She found her mother in the living room.

"Where's Mike?" Charlotte demanded.

"Wah, why are you sounding so accusing?" Mom asked. "It's not like I hit him over the head with a shovel and tied him to a chair in the garage."

"What sort of shows have you been watching lately?"

"Just the ones you like."

"Where is he?"

"Why are you so worried? He said he wanted some fresh air, so he went for a walk. Maybe an hour ago?"

An hour. That was a pretty long walk.

And yes, she was worried, because she knew this weekend had been tough for him. God, she never should have told him about her parents' invitation.

Sure, he'd been cheerful with her parents and they'd had fun on the beach. Because that was the kind of guy Mike was.

But there were other things, which he didn't talk about as much. He had with her, but she doubted that was common for him.

She hurried to the front hall and shoved her feet into her shoes.

"Where are you going?" Mom asked. "He'll be back soon."

"I need to find him."

"Don't you want your coffee?"

But Charlotte was already closing the door.

[26]

CHARLOTTE WAS PRETTY sure she knew where to find Mike, so she didn't bother texting.

Indeed, he was right where she'd expected. Under the willow tree on the outskirts of town. She could see his legs from several meters away, but apparently, he didn't see her approach; when she ducked under the branches, he startled.

"You found me," he said.

"Yeah. I know you." She sat beside him.

"I'm sorry. I was going to head back soon. I told your mom—"

"She said you were out for a walk, but I was worried about you, so I didn't want to wait. I didn't even have my coffee."

"We should rectify that." He started to stand, but she pulled him back down.

"No, let's talk here. Are you okay? Are we okay? I'm sorry I brought you here for the weekend. I can tell it's been hard."

"I couldn't sleep much last night, and it wasn't because of the twin bed."

"I saw you stick your head out the window," she said. "To see your old room?"

"Yes. I thought you were asleep."

"I was awake briefly."

He took both of her hands in his. "I love you, Charlotte," he said solemnly. "I realized it this morning, but perhaps I'd felt that way for a while. Perhaps I never stopped. I don't know—I'm not good at these things. And I'm not going to lie, it freaked me out. Especially back in this town, where it's easy to remember everything that was bad about my family. It's not usually so easy to hear my father's voice in my head. I've gotten much better at that over time. But here, knowing I love you… You know, I always thought you were too good for me."

She frowned. "Me? I don't even manage to put on pants most days—"

"I really don't see the problem here."

"And I'm, like, difficult. Cranky."

"Nah, not to me. I never thought that."

"I ran away when my ex-boyfriend proposed to me."

"It was justified."

"I like being alone."

"I like being alone on occasion, too," he said, "which is why I needed to get out of the house. Besides, you do like being with me some of the time, don't you?"

"Of course."

"You're so smart and pretty, and you always knew your own mind."

"Please don't put me on a pedestal. You'll just be disappointed."

"I'm not putting you on a pedestal," he said. "You can be a little difficult and cranky, alright? I just never cared. I always thought you were great. Sure, I got along well enough with the other kids at school, but I never seemed to do anything right, according to my family. I know it was bullshit, but it gets in your head, being told by the people who are supposed to love you that you'll never amount to anything. And so I spent years figuring things out." He paused. "For your sake, I want to be someone who knows all about love and relationships, but I'm not. I do get a little freaked out when I get close to someone, and I needed time to put my head on straight. To talk to a friend, my sister. People who will tell me not to be an idiot. I think I can do this. I want it more than anything. I just…maybe I'll need a little more therapy."

She squeezed his hands. "I love you, too. When I realized it, I knew you weren't ready to hear it yet, but you are now. I do love you, and it's been a long-ass time since I said that to anyone, and I never thought I'd say it to someone who eats cantaloupe on pizza—"

He cut her off by kissing her, and she wasn't complaining. He pulled her onto his lap and slipped his hands under the hem of her shirt. His hands were so warm and comforting, and they could do some pretty impressive shit, whether in bed or bent over her desk. He slid his tongue into her mouth, but it wasn't too much tongue, just the right amount.

"So, it's okay with you?" he said. "That I'm a bit of a work in progress?"

"Isn't everyone? I'm here for all of it with you. Neither of us is too good for the other. We're just…good for each other."

And then she kissed him again and thought of all the kisses they'd share in the future. There was so much to look forward to with him. Even if it wouldn't always be straightforward and easy, she knew he understood her better than anyone—she hadn't needed someone who was just like her—and he'd treat her the way she deserved to be treated. She'd do the same for him.

"I can't believe I found you again," he murmured, pressing a kiss to the base of her neck. "And I really can't believe you thought I was some lady-killer who was going to teach you fancy dating moves. But it brought us to this"—he pressed her closer to him—"so I'm not complaining. Now, let's find you some coffee before you get a headache from caffeine withdrawal."

"You sure you're ready to leave this hiding place?" She gestured at the slender branches.

"Yeah, I'm good now. I'm sorry I needed a little space this morning. I'm sorry I made you worry. I never intended for that to happen."

"It's fine, I get it."

"I promise, I'm in a better place now, and I'll talk to you about things. I want…" He clasped his hand in hers. "I want this to be my first and last proper relationship. No practice runs. There will be a few bumps as I get used to things, but—"

"I think you're doing a pretty great job."

And I want to end up with you, too.

"Before we go back to my parents' for coffee," she said, "I want to buy you a treat."

"A symbol of your undying devotion."

"If that's how you want to think of it, sure."

They walked across town, hand in hand. She led him into Ashton Corners Convenience & Video and opened up the freezer.

"Freezies before breakfast?" he asked.

"We're adults now, so we can do whatever the fuck we want. We're getting the big ones." She grabbed a blue one and a white one.

"I'm assuming the blue one is for you and the white one is for me."

"Obviously. What kind of flavor is white?"

"What kind of flavor is blue?"

"I think it's supposed to be blue raspberry," she said defensively.

"That tastes nothing like raspberry."

"Have you had it in the past twenty years? You probably haven't tasted a blue freezie since you proclaimed you liked white best when you were, like, six."

"Not true."

"Fine, I'll be generous, and you can try mine."

He did, and he still claimed it was a silly flavor.

It could only be expected from someone who liked Hawaiian pizza and sweet cider…someone who made her laugh by doing the Macarena at a steampunk bar…someone who had the best smile in the world, and the best biceps, and the best—

"You should probably eat your freezie before it melts," Mike said as they walked, knocking his hip against hers.

She had a bite of her icy, sugary blue raspberry freezie.

It tasted nothing like raspberry, but she didn't tell Mike.

By the time they returned to the house, they'd finished their freezies, and though she was in her thirties, Charlotte felt like she'd done something naughty.

There was coffee in the coffeepot. She poured herself a mug and sat down at the kitchen table, where her mother and father were reading the paper, because yes, they still got the paper delivered every day.

"Ah, good," Mom said. "You're both back. So nice to have company in the morning." She looked down at the paper, then glanced up again. "I meant to ask you. Did you hear any weird noises last night? I thought I heard a strange squeaking around eleven."

Charlotte was too horrified to speak.

Mike, however, said easily, "I did. I think it was a bird. I used to hear it sometimes when we lived next door."

"Sounded different from any bird I'd heard before. Must have known you were here."

Charlotte suppressed a laugh.

"Yeah, it must have," Mike said.

Later that day, after more time with her parents and more time on the beach, they drove back to Toronto and had sex in a bed that did not squeak.

~

"Let me buy you a drink for your birthday," Nicole said. "Blackberry nectarine cider?"

Charlotte made a face.

"You can share my Brussels sprouts," Sierra said.

"Haha, very funny," Charlotte said.

"We'll sing you 'Happy Birthday,' right here in the bar."

"You wouldn't dare."

Charlotte's parents had called earlier and sang to her. That was more than enough for the day.

Mike had said he would do something for her birthday tomorrow.

But he was here with her friends at Ossington Cider Bar tonight, as was Victor. Amy and Victor had gone on a short honeymoon to the Finger Lakes before she went back to school.

And then there were Nicole, Sierra, and Rose.

Julie came over to their table with a tray full of drinks.

"Here's your bone-dry cider, Charlotte, and your passionfruit peach cider, Mike. Happy birthday, dear sister."

"Happy birthday to you, too," Charlotte said. "Now can we forget about birthdays for the rest of the night? I've had quite enough."

"Happy birthday, darling," Mike murmured in her ear, and it made her skin prickle.

Yes, it was her birthday today. She was thirty-three.

At her very first birthday party, she'd apparently been so uncomfortable with everyone singing that she'd stuck her head in the cake and ruined her fussy pink dress.

And more than two months ago, she'd been at this bar with her friends and had run into Mike. She'd proposed that he teach her how to date, and now they were together for real.

Even for Charlotte Tam, it was hard not to feel a little sentimental when it was her birthday and she was surrounded by her friends and her wonderful boyfriend, who was now stroking her thigh under the table.

She was, coincidentally, wearing the outfit she'd worn on her first practice date with Mike: the pink shirt with the bow, jeans, and brown blazer. It wasn't like she had tons of nice clothes for going out, after all, though she did go out more often these days.

"Can I try your cider?" Mike asked.

"Sure, but you won't like it." She slid over her glass.

He had a sip and made a rather comical face. "How can you drink that stuff?"

She grabbed his passionfruit peach cider and had a sip. "I think I just got a cavity. If I'm going to have sugar, I'm eating cake or ice cream instead. Or a blue freezie."

"We should go to Treatzz later. Get you some fig goat cheese ice cream."

"Good idea. You can have the olive oil ice cream."

"Very funny."

"I never thought I'd say this, Charlotte, but you're cute when you're in a relationship." Rose had a faraway smile on her face. "I wonder who will be next to fall in love?"

"You," Nicole said immediately, then returned to checking out the muscled guy at the table next to them.

"I doubt it," Rose said. "Maybe you."

"Me? You know I don't date."

"Perhaps you just need a practice boyfriend to change your mind."

"A practice boyfriend? Ha!"

"You know," Sierra said, "I've actually started seeing someone."

"You have?" Amy said. "Why is this the first I'm hearing about it? What's his name?"

Amy, Nicole, and Rose continued to interrogate Sierra—who refused to give any details—while Charlotte turned her attention to the man next to her.

"Is there going to be more ice cream tomorrow?" she asked him. "Or cake?"

"You'll just have to wait and see."

The next morning, after Charlotte had drunk only a single coffee, Mike said it was time to leave. They took the subway to Spadina.

Charlotte had a feeling she knew where they were going.

Sure enough, they soon walked up to the sprawling Victorian that housed Nautilus.

"But it's only eleven," she said. "The sign says it opens at noon."

Mike just smiled at her and knocked on the door.

A man in a top hat answered. "You may head upstairs, Mr. Guo."

They walked through the empty bar, passing the hot air balloons and blimp. Up on the second floor, they walked through the science lab, where no drinks were currently being concocted, and past the velvet curtain, behind which they'd had their first kiss.

Mike led her to the top floor, to the room with the impressive steampunk coffeemaker. They were met by a woman wearing a long skirt, a corset, a white blouse, and a little hat with gears.

She curtsied and motioned to a table by the window. "It will be ready in just a moment."

They sat down at the table, and the woman brought over two lattes. Both mugs had raised designs on the outside: Charlotte's was a hot air balloon, and Mike's was a kraken. There was also a plate of scones with clotted cream and jam.

"I'll be in the back if you need me," the woman said, curtsying again.

Mike took Charlotte's hand in his. "What do you think? We get to keep the mugs. Figured you could use a mug that didn't have a bad geology pun, as awesome as those are."

She looked around. A quiet morning in a steampunk bar/tea salon, with a latte instead of tea. Just her and Mike.

"It's wonderful," she said, then reached for a blueberry scone.

"Nobody is going to sing for you, I promise."

She smiled at him, then broke off a piece of her scone and popped it in her mouth. "Mmm, that's delicious. I think I might love you."

"*Might*, she says."

She'd told him that she loved him several times over the past week. It was so natural to love him now, even if it hadn't been long.

She had another bite of her scone and moaned.

"Okay, you've gotta stop doing that," Mike said.

"If you insist." She let out a world-weary sigh and sipped her latte.

Then, as she held his gaze, she bit her lip, exactly as he'd taught her all those weeks ago.

Well, first she bit her upper lip, which made him laugh, and then she bit her lower lip as she tilted her head to the side.

"Come here," he said, his voice husky. "Or I'll start doing the Macarena."

As funny as that would be, she'd prefer to kiss him instead, and since there was nobody else in the room, she climbed onto his lap.

He gently cupped her cheeks before setting his lips to hers. He kissed her as though she was the best thing that had ever happened to him. As though he would always take care of her and knew she would take care of him in return.

Yes, he'd drag her out of the apartment and get her to do crazy things like go on a swan boat, but as she'd discovered, a little more time out in the world could be enjoyable with him by her side. She trusted him to hold her heart, and all her weird idiosyncrasies, with care.

She also trusted him to give her some damn good orgasms.

"We should drink our lattes before they get cold," she said.

"Good point." But he just kept kissing her instead.

And since she loved kissing him so much, she decided she could wait a little longer to ingest some caffeine.

Yep, this was love.

[EPILOGUE]

A few weeks later...

"RISE AND SHINE!" Mike said.

"Fuck off," Charlotte muttered, covering her head with a pillow.

He wasn't insulted. It was five thirty in the morning on a Saturday, after all.

Time for Plan B.

He grabbed the kraken mug full of coffee that he'd placed on his dresser and waved it under her nose. She perked up a bit but stayed lying down.

"You promised," he said.

"You're right. I did." She sat up, and with an eagerness that still made him laugh, she took the mug from his hand.

"It's decaf."

"Don't fuck with me."

Nah, he would never bring her decaf coffee at five thirty in the morning.

Once Charlotte had finished her coffee, they headed to his kitchen. He'd already started getting out the ingredients for their turkey dinner, which he was very excited about, even if it meant he had to wake up at an ungodly hour. They'd be eating in the early afternoon, since Julie had to work tonight and Charlotte's parents were coming in just for the day.

He'd never had the big turkey meal for Thanksgiving as a child, and he'd always wanted one. Thanksgiving was on Monday, but he was hosting it today for Charlotte's family, as well as Angela and Bailey, who were taking the train down from Ottawa this morning.

So, it would be better than any Thanksgiving turkey meal he could have had as a kid, since it was only with people who were important to him and treated him well.

Most notably, Charlotte.

In his childhood, he'd felt like love was conditional, and he'd never been good enough to earn it, even briefly. But he didn't have to be perfect to be worthy, and Charlotte loved him for who he was. It was a sign of how far he'd come that he could truly believe that. She'd been a constant in his life when he was younger, and now, he didn't ever want to let her go.

After her second cup of coffee and a quick bowl of cereal, she started cutting up the vegetables for the dressing. Mason had provided Mike with the recipes he used for dressing and cranberry sauce. Charlotte said cranberry sauce from a can was sufficient, but Mike wanted to make this a holiday to remember, and so he was using his friend's recipe, which had orange zest and other things in addition to cranberries and sugar.

Once they got the turkey in the oven, only ten minutes behind schedule, Mike placed his hands on Charlotte's hips and pulled her toward him. She still had sex hair from last night, and there was a small piece of celery in it.

"Hey, beautiful." He slid one hand to her ass and brought her against him, nuzzling the base of her neck. "I think we can take a little break from the kitchen now."

"Good idea. I have to run some inversions for work—"

"You didn't bring your computer with you," he said, calling her bluff.

And then she dragged him into the bedroom, where they made her sex hair even wilder.

~

That afternoon, they all sat around Mike's dining room table. With seven people, it was a little cramped, but he didn't mind. Charlotte had just finished carving the turkey, and there was a platter of meat in the center of the table, as well as dressing, potatoes, cranberry sauce, gravy, and salad. After their late lunch, there would be pie, coffee, and tea.

"This is so delicious." Bonnie stuffed a bite of turkey smothered in gravy in her mouth. "Very nice of you to have us over for Thanksgiving, Mike. You are such a good cook."

"It was a team effort." He patted Charlotte's shoulder.

"You're the one who chose the menu," she said.

"And you're the one who got rid of the spider. That was a very important job."

For the first time since the summer, Mike had found a spider in his apartment, and fortunately, his private spider-removal service had been present when he screamed.

"What kind of spider?" Bailey asked.

"Nothing venomous, don't worry," Charlotte said.

Bailey frowned.

"Tough luck, kid," Angela said, patting her back.

Bailey had recently expanded her interests to include venomous snakes. There was currently a watercolor of a king cobra on Mike's fridge, which was much better than a spider, even if this cobra could kill an elephant with one bite.

He wondered what sort of interests his and Charlotte's children would have. He would do his best to encourage them. It was a little way down the road, but he was looking forward to it. To his future with Charlotte.

~

After Thanksgiving dinner, Julie Tam sat at the table with her parents, a cup of tea clenched in her hands. Sadly, there was no booze in the tea.

"Isn't it so amazing?" Mom said. "Like something in a movie! They lived next door to each other as kids, and then they found each other twenty years later and fell in love."

"And he's a financial planner. This is a good job." Dad looked meaningfully at Julie.

Yeah, yeah. Julie's career—or lack thereof, in her parents' opinion—wasn't what they wanted. Plus, she lived with a room-mate and didn't have a boyfriend.

She'd heard it all before.

She glanced toward the kitchen, where Mike was washing dishes and Charlotte was drying. They'd refused to let anyone else help with the clean-up.

Mike splashed water droplets on Charlotte, and she shoved him lightly on the shoulder.

"Don't you dare," he said. "I'll hide your French press."

"As if you'd ever be stupid enough to do that."

And now they were kissing each other.

Julie was happy for her sister, even if Charlotte and Mike were sickeningly cute together. It was just that, well, Charlotte had always been the sister who gave their parents what they wanted. Even if some people might consider Charlotte a bit of a grouch, she was the one who'd gotten good grades in school. Her degree was more prestigious—in their parents' eyes—than Julie's. Their parents bragged about Charlotte being a self-employed geophysicist.

Now she had the perfect guy, too. Mom and Dad loved Mike, and the feeling was mutual.

Not that Julie's parents treated her like crap. They weren't mean people. It had just always been obvious that Charlotte was more accomplished in the ways they wanted. They believed Julie was capable, but she didn't want the sort of life they envisioned for her.

What would happen at Christmas? They'd probably all be back in Ashton Corners for a few days, and Julie would have to witness too much cuteness between Charlotte and Mike while her parents hinted—not at all subtly—that she should find a better job than working at a cider bar.

Ugh. Julie would need a plan to cope with that.

Perhaps she could surprise everyone by bringing home a neurosurgeon. Her parents would fawn all over him and forget about Julie's lack of respectable career.

The thought made her chuckle.

But, no.

She didn't want that to happen, even if it would be fun to see her family's reaction.

A strait-laced neurosurgeon—or another type of doctor or pharmacist—was the last person she'd date, right?

ABOUT THE AUTHOR

Jackie Lau decided she wanted to be a writer when she was in grade two, sometime between writing "The Heart That Got Lost" and "The Land of Shapes." She later studied engineering and worked as a geophysicist before turning to writing romance novels. Jackie lives in Toronto with her husband, and despite living in Canada her whole life, she hates winter. When she's not writing, she enjoys gelato, gourmet donuts, cooking, hiking, and reading on the balcony when it's raining.

To learn more and sign up for her newsletter,
visit jackielaubooks.com.

Cider Bar Sisters Series

Her Big City Neighbor

His Grumpy Childhood Friend

Her Pretend Christmas Date (novella)

Kwan Sisters/Fong Brothers Series

Grumpy Fake Boyfriend

Mr. Hotshot CEO

Pregnant by the Playboy

Holidays with the Wongs Series

A Match Made for Thanksgiving

A Second Chance Road Trip for Christmas

A Fake Girlfriend for Chinese New Year

A Big Surprise for Valentine's Day

Baldwin Village Series

One Bed for Christmas (prequel novella)

The Ultimate Pi Day Party

Ice Cream Lover

Man vs. Durian

Chin-Williams Series

Not Another Family Wedding

He's Not My Boyfriend